ABOUT THE AU

Bruce Kennard-Simpson was born in Torquay in 1929 and from a very early age surrounded himself with books. He became a passionate lifelong reader.

During World War 2, Bruce attended boarding school in Taunton and afterwards spent two years' National Service in the Royal Air Force, a time he thoroughly enjoyed.

Throughout his life, Bruce has written numerous novels, children's stories and poetry. *The Birth and Birth of Charley Johnson*, a biographical novel, was published by Austin Macauley in 2021 and this, *The Adventures of Captain Horatio Catte*, is one of his fondest works as it was written originally for his five children back in the 1960s.

As well as his passion for writing, Bruce inherited his mother's talent for music and composed many pieces for the piano. His playing has been featured on national radio.

In 1972 after a successful business career, Bruce purchased and renovated a beautiful Queen Ann period hotel in East Devon and ran this as a family business for over 20 years prior to his retirement. He continued to write and compose music into his early 90s.

Bruce Kennard-Simpson. 29th March 1929 – 24th March 2022

DEDICATION

This book is dedicated to my wonderful family – my wife, children, and grandchildren who have inspired me throughout my life.

Bruce Kennard-Simpson

The Adventures of Captain Horatio Catte

Illustrated by Kate Smith

AUSTIN MACAULEY PUBLISHERS™

LONDON • CAMBRIDGE • NEW YORK • SHARJAH

A CIP catalogue record for this title is available from the British Library.

ISBN 9781528931434 (Paperback)
ISBN 9781528936828 (ePub e-book)

www.austinmacauley.com

First Published 2023

Austin Macauley Publishers Ltd®
1 Canada Square
Canary Wharf
London
E14 5AA

ACKNOWLEDGEMENTS

My greatest thanks to Kate Smith, my lovely granddaughter, for her creativity and wonderful illustrations throughout this book.

I also wish to thank my son-in-law, Peter Astbury, for his invaluable help in bringing this book to production.

The Adventures of
CAPTAIN HORATIO CATTE

CAPTAIN CATTE'S ARMY

Chapter 1

THE TERRIBLE BARON Garvil lived in a huge castle built on a hill in the fair land of Merridew County. A forbidding tower rose out of the courtyard surrounded by grey walls, and was protected by a deep moat.

The Baron had tricked his old guardian, when he lay very ill, to give him the formula to produce a cheese which had the magical properties of eternal youth. Anyone eating it regularly would never grow old!

The Baron knew he could sell it in great quantities, which would make him very rich.

By using his power to threaten the local farmers, they had unwillingly agreed to sell him their milk cheaply to make his wonderful cheese – with the exception of the Mayor of the County. He had the biggest herd of cows in the land, but firmly refused to sell his milk to the Baron.

Now, because of his pride, the Baron was determined to overcome the Mayor, a happy man with a lovely family, particularly Belinda, his beautiful daughter.

One night, the evil Baron and Raikes, his chief henchman, were sitting in the imposing dining hall with its great granite walls. Now, you'll want to know what these two bad men looked like.

Baron Garvil was very large, and his face was squarish, with untidy black hair, matched by a black beard. He had beetling eyebrows and piercing, glowering eyes.

Raikes was a short, thin-faced man with foxy eyes, and at all times obeyed his cruel master, who was sitting drinking large quantities of ale.

"Raikes!" roared the Baron suddenly. "Something very unpleasant must be done to this meddlesome Mayor! I must have his milk!"

Raikes shrank back in his seat.

"We've tried lots of your clever ideas," sneered the Baron, "but none of them have worked."

Raikes coughed nervously. "There is, of course, Belinda, his daughter. She is a lovely girl, and he's more fond of her than of anything else."

After a thoughtful pause, the Baron leered, "It would be a great pity if anything happened to such a sweet little girl, wouldn't it? She needs to be put somewhere very safe, eh? Don't you think the Great Tower would be ideal for such a purpose?"

Chapter 2

IT WAS SUCH a beautiful morning that Belinda decided to go out for a walk along a leafy lane to a peaceful glade, one of her favourite places. She was accompanied, as nearly always, by Mrs Jones, a large ginger cat.

On her way, Belinda came upon a gypsy caravan standing in a clearing, with a shaggy pony still between the shafts. Beside the caravan paced a man, wringing his hands in agitation.

"Oh, what am I going to do?" he kept repeating over and over again. The kind-hearted Belinda was upset to see him in such a state.

"Please," she beseeched him, "let me help you."

"Oh, I wish you could," he replied hopefully. "My father is ill in there, and just lies there and groans."

"Now, don't you worry! I'll go in and have a look at him."

Belinda hurried up the wooden steps and into the caravan.

It was quite dark inside, but she could make out a bunk in the corner, with someone lying under some blankets. Gently, she crept towards it and lifted the covers from the man's face.

"Ohhh - !" she gasped, as suddenly he sat up and grabbed her. The door banged shut, and immediately the caravan began to move. Raikes - for it was he who had been outside - had sprung onto the driving seat and whipped up the pony.

Belinda was in the hands of the wicked Baron!

Chapter 3

INSIDE THE CARAVAN, the terrified Belinda was powerless.

"It's useless for you to struggle," cried the Baron. "You can't get away, and no-one can hear you if you shout. I'm not going to hurt you, my dear. I'm just going to keep you hostage until I've concluded some business with your father."

He gave an evil chuckle. "I'm sure he'll want his little girl back again as soon as possible!"

Now, it was part of Baron Garvil's plan that no-one would know what had happened to Belinda, but someone had seen it all! It was Mrs Jones the cat!

When the caravan had moved off, she realised that Belinda was inside. With her sharp instinct for danger, Mrs Jones was sure that some evil had befallen her mistress. She sprang after the caravan and, with a great leap, landed on its steps.

Using her sharp claws, she scrambled up until she could peer through the window. She saw the Baron holding Belinda and knew that she was in danger.

Now, Mrs Jones was a very intelligent cat. She decided that she would hide herself, and find out where they were going.

Chapter 4

THE MAYOR AND his wife were accustomed to Belinda going for a walk on her own, as she usually had a following of friendly animals, and no evil was expected in Merridew.

Into Belinda's home burst Mrs Jones, covered in mud and fighting for breath, as she had run a long way.

"Mrs Jones, wherever have you been?" gasped the Mayor's wife. "You're filthy! Have you been chasing birds?"

Of course, Mrs Jones could not talk, but she had an idea how she could tell her shocking news. She snatched a ribbon from the sewing box and twisted it around her own head. Then she stood on her hind legs and successfully copied the way Belinda walked.

"It's Belinda!" cried the Mayor. "Something has happened to her! Please, Mrs Jones, try to show us what it is!"

Very cleverly, Mrs Jones ran to Mrs Mayor, caught her hand and tried to pull her away.

"She's been kidnapped, hasn't she?" demanded the Mayor. "If only we knew where she has been taken!"

Mrs Jones gave a loud miaow and ran away from them, then turned to show that they must follow her.

"Look," cried the Mayor, "she knows where Belinda is, and wants us to follow her. Come on – be quick!"

Chapter 5

WITH MRS JONES LEADING the way, they ran off through the woods until they reached the castle. The drawbridge was raised, so they could go no further.

But while they were pondering how to rescue Belinda, a great voice boomed above them. It was the wicked Baron, leaning out of one of the castle windows.

"Good evening, Mr and Mrs Mayor! What brings you to my humble abode?" he said mockingly, with an ugly smile on his face.

"We know that you have kidnapped our daughter Belinda, and you are holding her in your castle!" shouted the Mayor furiously.

"You sound just like a policeman!" jeered the Baron.

"Just hand her over to us this instant," said the Mayor angrily, "or I'll make trouble for you."

The Baron glowered. "If you were more friendly," he growled, "and sold me all your milk, like the other farmers, then you might find that your dear little daughter would return home to you."

The Mayor was fuming. "So that's what you're after, is it? Well, you won't get me to sign, and I'll see you are punished for your wickedness."

"Ho, ho!" laughed the Baron, then he snarled, "Go home, you silly little man, and think about it. You won't beat me!"

The Mayor shook his fist at the Baron, and his wife hurried him away. It was a very sad and angry party that made its way home.

Chapter 6

O N REACHING HOME they sat in silence, not knowing what to do to free their daughter, without letting the Baron have the milk he wanted. But clever Mrs Jones had a good idea.

She crept away unnoticed and made her way to the cellars, where she turned towards a dark corner. There was a door, and above it a forbidding notice:

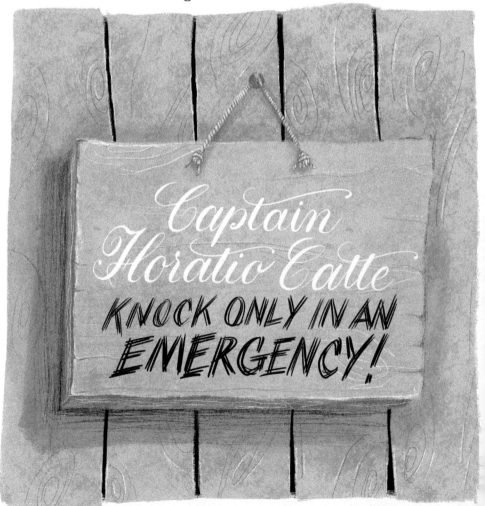

Captain
Horatio Cattle
KNOCK ONLY IN AN
EMERGENCY!

Her fear for Belinda's safety was excuse enough for her to use the big black knocker on the door.

A shutter opened and a gruff voice enquired, "What do you want? It had better be important to disturb me at this time of night."

"Oh sir, I am so worried!" cried Mrs Jones in great distress. "Belinda, the Mayor's daughter, has been kidnapped by the terrible Baron Garvil, and he's hidden her in his castle!

"You are the only one who will know how to rescue her," she finished.

Captain Catte opened the door and took Mrs Jones into his snug little den, where two armchairs stood in front of a blazing wood fire. On the walls hung pictures of Captain Catte and his ancestors.

The Captain was an imposing figure. He was tall, and stood upright, as often did Mrs Jones, due to associating so much with humans.

He was obviously used to command. His fur was ginger, and he wore an officer's uniform, with a gold braided belt, from which hung a sword in its scabbard.

Despite his military appearance, the Captain was a kindly person. He could see that Mrs Jones was very upset, and spoke gently to her.

"Come, my dear, and sit by the fire. You shall tell me what all this is about."

Mrs Jones thanked him and told him the full story. He did not interrupt, but his deep frown showed his concern.

When she had finished, he sat in silence for a while. Then he turned towards her.

"Well, my dear lady," he said, "I am sure that Belinda is not in any danger, as she is too valuable to the Baron as a hostage. She is the only means he has of getting what he wants from her father."

Then he went on to say, "I think it is best now if you return to the family, and I will let you know what I decide."

When she had gone, he settled down to think. He would have to call a Council of War!

Chapter 7

ONE OF THE landmarks of Merridew was a great oak tree. It was hundreds of years old. Captain Catte had played in it when he was very young, and had interwoven twigs so that, as they grew, they formed a thick floor in the boughs. He had also fashioned a rough table out of wood.

This had always been a secret place for the Captain when he wanted to make his plans, and it was also the meeting place of the Council of Cats.

It was to this tree that he now made his way.

As he reached the platform, a big black crow swooped down and landed on the table.

"Aha! So there you are, Sinbad," the Captain greeted him. "I was hoping you'd be here. I have a task for you."

The crow cocked his head, his piercing eyes watching Captain Catte closely.

"We are faced with the greatest crisis ever to come upon Merridew," the Captain explained. "It's going to take all our time and thought to solve it. It is vital to call a Council of Cats immediately. So be off with you, and look sharp!"

With a great flapping of wings, Sinbad soared out of sight.

There were many reasons why a bird should be the

Captain's messenger. Sinbad could cover a great distance quickly, and his sharp eyes could see a long way.

The members of the Council were spread far and wide, and as Sinbad ranged over the county, he gave an especially raucous cry.

This advised the Council members that an important emergency had arisen, and that they should attend a meeting without delay.

Each cat in turn raced off towards the tree. Soon they all arrived, and every available space was occupied.

Captain Catte waited until all the members of the Council were assembled, then took up his position in the centre of the platform, and waited for silence.

"We have a grave problem on our hands," he said. "You all know Belinda, the lovely daughter of the Mayor of Merridew. Well, she's been kidnapped!"

A loud murmur of distress arose from the Council.

The Captain told them that she was now in the hands of the evil Baron, and imprisoned in the castle's turret room.

This was greeted with hisses of anger. They wished to set out there and then to attack the castle, but they listened to what the Captain had to say.

"You will get your chance in due course," he promised them. "I have a plan!"

"Ahhh!" they purred in anticipation.

Chapter 8

"WE MUST ACT carefully," said Captain Catte, "so that Belinda will be placed in no danger. The Baron must not suspect our plans."

He stopped for a long drink of refreshing milk, then he continued, "We will start by making war on our old friends – the mice!"

This news was greeted by roars (if they could be called that) of approval from the Councillors.

The Captain went on, "I know we haven't seen action against them for months, but this time, none of them must be hurt."

There were howls of dismay from the cats.

"Now just you listen to me," Captain Catte said sharply. "I don't want them hurt, but I do want them terrified, so that they'll run away in panic, looking for somewhere safe to hide.

"When you chase them, it's most important that they head towards the castle," he explained. "They must all take refuge in the cellars – they can get in through the drains which run under the moat."

The Captain paused, then went on, "After a while, they'll become hungry, and start looking for food. And what is it," he asked, "that mice particularly like to eat?"

"CHEESE!" yelled the cats, with huge grins.

"Exactly!" agreed the Captain. "And there's no doubt that

in a very short time, there'll be none of the Baron's valuable stocks of special cheese left. Then, he'll be as poor as a church mouse!"

The cats were struck by the funny side of this, and they rolled around the platform with mirth.

Captain Catte gave them time to recover from their amusement, then he cleared his throat loudly, at which they again fell silent.

"That is all I have to tell you for the moment, but it will give you plenty to do. This meeting is now closed."

Chapter 9

WITHOUT DELAY, THE war against the mice got underway.

Chased by the cats, they were in headlong flight, seeming to be running in every direction – but they were not!

All the paths they took led to the moat, where the frantic mice disappeared into the drains leading to the castle. Captain Catte stood on the path between the village houses and shops, making certain that the battle went the way he intended.

As he watched, there was a great cry of anger, which came from within the clockmaker's shop. In his need to escape, a mouse had scampered across his bench. A large black cat chased after him, and in doing so, upset a tin of luminous paint.

The mouse, the cat and the tin of paint shot through the door, closely followed by the irate clockmaker.

Captain Catte watched in amusement as they disappeared into the distance. He did not know it at the time, but this episode was to prove very important in the coming assault on the castle.

Chapter 10

BARON GARVIL SAT by the table, gazing angrily into the distance. His plan didn't seem to be working. No one had come from the Mayor to plead for Belinda's release.

He had sent Raikes up to the battlements several times, hoping he would report the approach of a party with a white flag of surrender, but all Raikes had seen were hundreds of cats running around the fields.

"Huh, spring fever, I suppose," he muttered, and promptly forgot them.

The Baron leaned forward in his great wooden chair, and raised the flagon of ale to his lips. It was empty.

"RAIKES!" he bellowed, "get me some beer from the cellar – and be quick about it!"

Raikes ran to the cellar door to escape his master's wrath.

"Right away, sir!" he cried, almost falling down the steps in his haste. He caught the lantern he was carrying against the rough wall and broke it. Now he was in complete darkness!

As his eyes became used to it, he realised that he was not alone – he was being watched by hundreds of gleaming eyes! And he could hear rustling and whispering sounds from all around.

With a cry of terror, he ran blindly back up the cellar steps, slammed the door behind him, and leant against it, panting with fear.

All this commotion had been heard by the Baron, who

stormed along the passage. He saw the panic-stricken Raikes.

"What on earth are you doing, Raikes?" he yelled. "And where is my beer?" He caught Raikes by the scruff of the neck.

"What's happened to you, you horrible little man?"

"It – it's in th-the cellar, sir," stammered Raikes, shivering with fright.

"What is?" snarled his master.

"I dunno, sir! Hundreds of little eyes staring at me – like lots of tiny ghosts – it's horrible!"

"Ghosts! Pah! I'll soon show you! Get your lantern."

Raikes cringed. "I c-can't, sir, I b-broke it."

"Aren't you a little coward! Go and get another, immediately! This time I'm going down there... and you're coming with me."

Reluctantly, Raikes went off to find another lamp. On his return, the Baron led the way down the cellar steps with great caution. Something must have frightened his henchman, who was not easily scared.

They reached the floor of the cellar. Raikes shone the light all around, but there was no sign of anyone or anything.

Chapter 11

"WELL, WELL, YOUR little ghostly friends seem to have gone home, don't they? Perhaps the sight of you frightened them away!" said the Baron with heavy sarcasm. "You can see the cellar's empty."

Yet something was different! Suddenly it struck him – the cellar was certainly completely empty! He gave a great shout of dismay.

"Raikes, there's nothing here! All my cheese has been stolen! I'm ruined!" he wailed.

"But who could have done it, sir?" stuttered Raikes. "The drawbridge is still up, and all the gates are closed. How could anyone get in – or out, carrying all that cheese?"

Just then, there was a movement in the corner, and a little furry creature with a bulging tummy scuttled across the cellar and disappeared down a drain.

"There's the thief!" cried the Baron. "Those – and thousands more – were the eyes that frightened you. That's why all those cats were outside – they were chasing mice!"

He strode up and down, waving his arms in desperation.

"All my special magic cheese – gone!" he bellowed. "I'll never be able to build it up again. It took years and years!"

He grabbed a flagon of beer, stamped upstairs, and sank into his chair.

"Oh, it's no use, I can't think tonight," he muttered hopelessly. He emptied his flagon, and presently snores rent the air.

The Baron was asleep.

Chapter 12

THE NEXT MORNING, Baron Garvil awoke, rose, and peered fearfully into the cellar, hoping it had all been a bad dream. But it had all been true.

Wearily, he climbed up to the battlements of the castle and scanned the fields, but there were no cats to be seen.

Then his face grew red with anger – there were hundreds of mice, sleeping on their backs, their little open mouths giving out contented snores. Their fat, cheese-filled tummies were warming in the sun.

In the past the evil Baron would have roared out after them, intent on destroying, but it seemed pointless now, and somehow he hadn't the energy.

But if it all seemed quiet to the Baron, this was misleading. Back in his den, the Captain was working out the next phase of his attack on the castle.

The table in front of him was covered in history books, showing battles of long ago. As yet, no plan had come to him, until his eye fell upon the design of a monster catapult. This had been used for hurling great metal balls into enemy positions.

He certainly had no cannon balls, so what could he shoot into the castle? Suddenly he remembered something he had seen earlier, when the mice were being chased.

The more he thought about the idea, the more delighted he became. He raced to the meeting tree and sent the crow off on an urgent mission. He summoned the Council so that he could explain his cunning and original plan.

Soon they all had their orders and knew exactly what they must do. The attack would begin at midnight!

Chapter 13

AS DARKNESS DESCENDED on Merridew County, several groups of cats crept into the forest near the castle. One group searched along the edge of the wood for young saplings which would bend without breaking.

These saplings were forced over until their tops touched the ground, then they were pegged down, and left. There must have been at least fifty of them.

Another group pulled behind them a wooden cart on which was a huge barrel with a tap at the end. This was hard work, and the cats grumbled as they heaved it into a clearing.

Once there, directed by the Captain, they hauled the barrel up with ropes and dropped it onto a trestle, with the tap facing into the clearing. Lined up on the grass stood the elite of the army, who had been chosen to be in the firing line when the assault took place.

Hidden amongst the trees were the support troops, while yet another platoon of cats slunk away into the night and took up their positions for a very special task.

All were now ready awaiting the signal to start the most fantastic attack of all time.

"Right, men," said the Captain quietly, "you will now march slowly and noiselessly past the barrel."

The tap was turned gently and, as they passed under it,

each cat became covered from head to paws with the luminous paint contained in the barrel.

In turn, they left the clearing and took up positions so that each cat stood beside one of the saplings which, you will remember, had been bent double.

On a word of command from the Captain, an arrow, also covered with luminous paint, shot high into the air so that all could see it.

At this signal, the whole army of cats hidden amongst the trees began to wail, as often cats do at night, singing to the moon.

It was a hideous sound, enough to scare even the bravest of people.

Chapter 14

IN THE CASTLE, the bad Baron, worn out by his troubles, slept soundly. In nearby rooms slept Raikes and the rest of the Baron's men. Snores told of their deep sleep, and all was peaceful.

But not for long!

Suddenly there was an ear-piercing, unearthly noise! The Baron shot up in bed, quivering with fear. Raikes sat up, clutching his sheets to his chin, while the others burrowed under the bedclothes.

The noise grew louder and louder, until the Baron could stand it no longer, and leapt from his bed. He ran along the corridor, shouting to his men to get up and follow him.

Although they were frightened by the unearthly noise, they were also scared of the Baron, and obeyed him. He rushed up the steps to the parapet of the castle, followed by Raikes and the others.

Out there in the open the noise was deafening, and as they gazed towards the forest, they saw a sight which froze them in horror.

As the wailing increased, Captain Catte kept a close watch on the castle for any reaction. When the Baron and his men appeared, he gave a grin of satisfaction. This was what he had been waiting for.

"Load!" he shouted, whereupon each chosen member of the assault force lay on a sapling, and clung on tightly.

"FIRE!" he yelled, and beside each of these saplings, a cat

pulled out the pegs, releasing the young trees. These shot up like uncoiled springs, throwing the attackers high into the air towards the castle.

The Baron and his gang were terrified at the sight of large numbers of cats, glowing with luminous paint, hurtling through the dark night sky towards them. This was way too much – their nerves were shattered! They fled from the battlements.

Chapter 15

BELINDA, STILL SHUT up in the turret, was startled and very frightened by the noise until, with the whirring of wings, Sinbad the crow landed on her window sill and solemnly winked at her.

Her fears finally disappeared when one of the glowing cats, whose tree had been more bendy than the others, overshot the battlements, and also landed on her window sill.

Belinda was now certain that they had come to rescue her.

In the middle of the battle, Mrs Jones had hurried back to the Mayor's house, where she ran from room to room, miaowing loudly to gain their attention, and showing them that they must follow her. They guessed it must be connected with Belinda.

As they neared the castle they heard the terrifying wailing, and were naturally frightened when they saw the cats flying through the air like shooting stars.

Baron Garvil and his men wanted to escape from that chaotic and awful attack as soon as possible. The Baron ran in panic to the stables, where a coach always stood ready for use. The rest followed him.

Jumping onto the driver's seat of the coach and taking up a long whip, the Baron drove the horses at full speed through the gates and over the drawbridge, which had been lowered, and onto the lane outside.

We must now remember the other force which the Captain had kept for a special task – one which would bring the whole campaign to a successful end.

Following the orders of Captain Catte, these cats lay down in the lane, one behind the other, six feet apart, facing the castle entrance. Behind the last cat were the cliffs, and below them, the sea!

Chapter 16

THE BARON CROUCHED over the reins, cracking the whip, and making the horses gallop ever faster. Without realising it, he followed the line of cats' eyes which shone in the coach's lamps.

Suddenly the Baron, his men, the coach and horses, were flying through the air. They had driven at breakneck speed right over the cliffs, just as the Captain had intended.

With a great splash they hit the water, and disappeared from sight – a fitting end for such wicked people!

When it became known that the evil Baron and his gang were gone, there was great rejoicing in the castle.

The Mayor and his wife, guided by Belinda's cries, ran up the circular stone staircase inside the turret to the room where she was held prisoner. Luckily the key was in the lock outside, and they were soon holding their daughter in their arms, tears of joy running down their cheeks. At last, she was free!

Belinda told her parents all about her kidnap, and how she had been treated as a prisoner.

In the courtyard below, the task force – still glowing with the paint – were telling tales of their experiences and bravery to a crowd which listened in awe. What a wonderful army they were, and what a victory they had won!

The Captain watched them with amusement, and pride, for he had trained them to do a good job.

At length, he turned quietly away and strolled back to his

den. There, to his surprise, stood Mrs Jones. She wanted to thank him, because she had been the only one who knew his plan.

How could the others know, being only humans? But he didn't want any praise. He looked down at her, offered her his paw, and said with a smile, "Let's both of us have a nice cup of tea!"

But that wasn't the end of it. That night a celebration party was held, with feasting and dancing. Everyone was happy – and thankful for the successful outcome of Captain Catte's plan.

The party was in full swing; there was much laughter and merriment. Until... four figures, dripping water onto the floor, appeared before them. Their clothes were soaking, and so were they!

A horrified silence fell on the party. They recognised the Baron and some of his men, but something was different about them. The Baron stepped forward, humbly. He made for the Captain who eyed him sternly. "What do you want?" he snapped.

"Your forgiveness, sir – for all I have done to you." He paused, then in subdued tones, he continued: "When we fell into the sea, at first I was angry... then I changed. The water seemed to wash all my evil thoughts away. We made for the shore and all of us felt happy – and free! Then we came here to put ourselves to your mercy."

No-one moved. Sadly, in silence, the Baron turned to leave.

"Wait!" Belinda moved towards him. She took his hands in hers. "You really have been very wicked." He hung his head in shame. "But I will forgive you, and welcome you all to join us... when you have been given some dry clothes!" she said, with a smile.

The joy on the faces of the Baron and his men was immense. Everyone followed the lead given by Belinda and the party continued well into the night.

Merridew County was never the same again!

CAPTAIN CATTE
AND THE
OCTOPUSES

Chapter 1

TWO LARGE CATS lay reclining in the sunshine along the thick branch of a big elm tree.

"Are you going to the meeting tonight at the old oak tree?" asked the tortoiseshell cat.

"What meeting?" enquired the other, an elegant Siamese.

"Didn't you know? Captain Catte has called it. It's very important – even Uncle Ebenezer will be there."

"What's it all about?" queried the Siamese.

"Nobody knows, but it must be very important for him to go."

"I'm surprised the old fool knows about anything but his books."

"You're right! And doesn't he think he's somebody! Never a kind word to say to anyone."

"Well, I suppose we'll have to go. What time is it?"

"Sharp at seven o'clock, at the meeting tree."

The tortoiseshell cat let out a howl of dismay.

"Seven o'clock! That means supper will be late. Honestly, there's no consideration these days. I shall be starving by then."

So saying, two pairs of eyelids closed heavily over two pairs of eyes as the cats fell into a heavy doze, and the only sound was a contented purr – in harmony. They were so deeply asleep that they didn't know that the time was passing and approaching the hour of the meeting, until they were very rudely awakened.

A great big black crow flew straight for their rear-quarters at speed, and speared both of them with a quick movement of his sharp beak. With howls of anguish, clutching their injuries, they fell from the branch onto the ground below.

"That horrible bird!" cried the Siamese cat. "I wish its wings would fall off!"

Sinbad the crow was good at his job, and always made sure that everyone attended any gatherings called by

Captain Catte, so the two outraged felines (posh name for cats) made their way quickly to the meeting tree.

Such was the hold that Captain Catte had over everyone, the meeting tree was alive with cats when the appointed hour arrived. A great buzz of cats' talk filled the air as they wondered what was so important that the Captain had called them all together.

Chapter 2

AT A LITTLE table sat the Captain, and beside him was Uncle Ebenezer, who looked as crotchety as ever. Presently the Captain rose to his feet and raised his arms in the air. A hush fell upon the gathering, and many leaned forward to hear him speak.

He began: "The first part of this meeting has not much to do with me. Uncle here," – he pointed to the figure beside him – "has a lot to say to you. When he has finished I will fulfil my part of this evening. I now call on Uncle Ebenezer to address you."

So saying, he resumed his chair.

Slowly, Uncle got to his feet, and for a while stood there casting his sharp eyes over them all. They began to feel a bit uneasy.

"You are all too fat!" he barked at them. They gasped. What on earth did he mean by that?

"Yes," Uncle continued, "I can see you are surprised, but it's true. You have all become fat and lazy. It wouldn't have done in my younger days, I can tell you." They groaned. The old idiot was going to lecture them on 'the younger generation'. They had heard it all before. It was all deadly boring!

One of the bolder cats rose to his feet.

"I'm not sitting here and listening to him," he said loudly.

"Oh yes you are!" snapped the old gentleman, waving his stick at the offender. "Sit down at once and take note of what I am going to say."

The cat sat down, muttering to himself.

"I intend to do something about your poor condition," said Uncle Ebenezer. "I have a plan which will give you a lot of hard work, some adventure, and a chance to see other lands. For some time, I have been studying the lives of tropical fish. I have read all I can about them, but it isn't enough. I want to go and see them, and I will need to take some of you along to assist me. I shall fit out a sailing ship, fill it with provisions, and on a good tide and in fair weather, I will set sail for the South Seas."

Uncle Ebenezer paused, then continued, "I will need a crew, and I will pick the strongest and best-tempered from amongst you for the purpose. Now, when I say I shall fit out a sailing ship, this means that you will build it!"

Cries of horror filled the air as the cats thought of all the hard work this would mean. And in any case, they had no idea how to make a ship.

At this point, Uncle Ebenezer sat down and Captain Catte took over the meeting, to give them information concerning the building of the ship. This task would mean that every member of the county would have to take part, because the workload was going to be very heavy.

The first thing to do was to find someone who knew about ships, and Captain Catte knew of just the right person. This was Captain Jabez, the owner of one of the most successful fishing smacks on those shores, and was famous for his voyages in the worst possible weathers. But what catches he brought in! Some of the fish were monsters – and quite as ugly!

Chapter 3

WHEN THE CAPTAIN went to see Jabez, he found the old salt sitting on a low stone wall beside the harbour, mending some nets, and quietly humming an old sea shanty to himself.

"Morning Jabez!" he called. "How are things with you?"

"Oh, middling fair, thank 'ee," was the reply, given without looking up from his task. "Don't often see you here. Doo 'ee want something?"

The Captain sat down on the wall beside him.

"As a matter of fact I do. I need your help." He paused, then slowly he added, "I want you to teach me how to build a ship."

At this, the surprised Jabez looked up sharply.

"Build a ship? Why would you need a ship, and where would 'ee be going?"

Captain Catte explained to the old sailor the reason for the voyage.

"My Uncle Ebenezer has, for a long time, been studying the lives of tropical fish, and although he's read all he can about them, he feels it isn't enough. He wants to go and see them in their natural homes. For that reason, he needs a strong ship to take him to the South Seas."

The old fisherman was delighted. He had not built a good-sized ship for many years, and could hardly wait to begin.

"'Tis going to be a stout vessel," he said thoughtfully. "You'll be travelling some rough old seas – I know because

I've seen 'em. It'll mean a tidy lot of timber, and ropes, and sailcloth. Oh yes, and plenty of pitch!"

He stood up suddenly, laying aside his nets. "Follow me!" he ordered Captain Catte, and set off along the quay at a brisk pace.

Presently, he stopped in front of a long stone building with two large doors. He produced a key from his pocket, and inserted it into the lock. It turned easily and he swung open one door and went inside.

The Captain followed him and gazed in awe at the contents. Proudly, Jabez watched him as he stood open-mouthed in wonder. It was crammed full of items of shipping. Great masts were stacked neatly along one of the walls, together with spars, coils of rope, and stacks of barrels. He had never dreamed that such a place existed in Merridew.

Jabez broke the silence. "I reckon there's well nigh a whole ship in here. Many years ago, most likely before you was born, I helped build ships. Great sailing ships they was, and as strong as iron. Never a one was lost at sea.

"Then no-one needed 'em any more, so all this gear was left. But 'tis alright though. 'Tis proper ship-shape fashion, as you can see."

The Captain had to agree with him. This would make the task much easier, but still a lot of effort would be required. Another thought struck him.

"What about a design? We have to know what we're going to need in timber and other things."

Jabez motioned him over to a large sea chest which stood in a corner. He opened it, and the inside was full of plans and charts. He riffled through them until he found the one he wanted, and spread it out on a long table.

"This'll be the one for 'ee," he said with satisfaction. The plan was of a three-masted ship, appearing large enough for their purpose. Captain Catte liked what he saw. It was obviously very strong.

"Can we make this?" he asked doubtfully.

"Oh, there's nought to it! Not if you knows what you'm about. Bless you, I've made many of 'em. Of course, we had proper craftsmen in them days, who knew their jobs, not like that lily-livered bunch you're going to use. But I'll learn 'em!" The latter was given in a real schoolmaster's voice.

"You send 'em down to me and I'll make 'em work – oh yes, until their whiskers drop off!"

Chuckling at the prospect, he led the way outside.

Chapter 4

IT WAS A very happy Captain Catte who made his way over to Uncle Ebenezer's cottage to give his report. His Uncle was delighted. They sat down for the rest of the day, making out work parties, not only to learn carpentry and sail-making from Jabez, but to collect the extra timber that would be needed. Luckily there was no shortage of wood, as forests ringed the County, and could do with thinning out.

Captain Jabez was now busy teaching the cats to use carpentry tools, not without accidents. Quite a number of cats sported bandages on heads or paws, where they had been in contact with saws and hammers, but they were improving. Soon he was able to put them to work on the ship.

The whole yard was a hive of activity, but amongst all the hustle and confusion, the ship gradually took shape, and all who were working on her found a new pride in what they were helping to create.

With the completion of the hull came the job of using the pitch to make it watertight. Quite a lot of it ended up on the cats and quayside, but enough was put on the ship to make it effective.

The stepping of the masts brought its problems, but eventually this was done, and next came the actual launching of the ship. This was a special occasion. No-one could remember a proper launching being carried out before, and the company of cats made the most of it. The band was called out, and very smart they were, having polished their instruments and pressed their uniforms.

The ladies had turned themselves out in their best gowns, and had produced a feast bigger and better than any that had been prepared over the years. Flags flew from all the ships' masts, and bunting was draped over the ropes. It was a magnificent sight!

The hour for the actual launch was at hand. A platform had been erected by the bows, and at the end of a bright ribbon was tied a bottle of the best milk the County could produce. But who was going to do the honours? It had not been mentioned by anyone. Surely it had not been forgotten?

Up onto the platform strode Captain Catte. He raised his paws, calling for silence. A hush fell over the crowd.

"My friends and fellow workers, I am proud of you! Just look at your handiwork! Isn't she beautiful? And now she is ready for her element – the sea." He seemed to look into the distance as if he was expecting something.

"Ah!" he said, and turned back to his audience. "If you look up the lane, you will see a coach approaching. I have taken the liberty of inviting a special guest to send our ship on its way."

The coach drew up at the foot of the platform, the door opened and out stepped Belinda, the much-loved human daughter of the human Mayor of Merridew.

"I ask you to greet our lovely Belinda, who is going to perform the launching ceremony." A loud cheer rang out as she ascended the platform, then everyone became quiet so that they might hear her speak.

"My very dear friends," she began, "this is the happiest day of my life! You have built this magnificent vessel, and will be setting out on a long and maybe dangerous voyage where none of you have been before. God speed to you all, and send you safely home to us. I name this ship "The Jabez", in honour of the man who made the building of it possible, and may God protect all that sail in her!" She took the bottle and sent it swinging on the end of the ribbon until it broke over the ship's bows.

Slowly, watched fearfully by all, the sturdy ship started to move. Gradually the pace quickened until, with a splash, it reached the ocean, there to ride proudly for all to see. A loud cheer went up from the crowd, whilst up on deck stood the ship's new commander, Captain Jabez.

Chapter 5

THE LAUNCHING OF the ship was not the end of the matter.

The next thing to be done was to fit her out. As she stood, she was just a hull with three bare masts. Obviously she was nowhere near ready for sea. Cross-beams, halyards, lanyards, sheets and sails all had to be fitted, and down by the quay, a workforce of cats swarmed over the vessel, carrying out a multitude of tasks.

Besides everything else, the victuals – that is, food and drink – had to be taken on board and stowed away safely in the hold. Because some of the seas would certainly be rough, everything had to be tied down to stop it moving about. Unless this was done, there was a real danger that the ship would capsize, and that would be the end of all of them!

Because of their favourite diet, most of the food was salted-down fish, and as the voyage was bound to be a long one, they had to be sure that enough was taken to last them. Captain Catte hoped that when they reached their destination they would find supplies with which to replenish their stocks, but this could not be relied upon.

Unfortunately, they would have to drink water, as milk certainly wouldn't last. The weather would most likely prove to be very hot once they entered the South Seas, and milk would have gone off.

Everything was now approaching completion, and one fine morning a party of lady cats walked down to the ship, each carrying a big laundry basket, piled high with snow-white sails. They had followed the progress of all the work with keen interest, and when they heard that lots of sails were needed, they saw their chance to help.

All the lady cats gathered together, and were shown by Jabez how to go about it. They soon learned, and happily went about their tasks. Now all the sails were complete. Their arrival was what the crew had been waiting for, and with a will they set about attaching them to the yard-arms, and furling them neatly until they would be needed.

Spare sets were stowed away in the sail lockers. During the voyage, some were bound to get ripped or even lost overboard, so there had to be replacements. This operation meant that everything was finished, and the 'Jabez' was now ready to put to sea.

Chapter 6

CAPTAIN CATTE, UNCLE Ebenezer and the crew were all impatient to begin the voyage, but Jabez wouldn't hear of it. Every morning he strode around the deck, taking a sniff of the air and searching the horizon for clouds. He had been a fisherman for many years and had a 'feel' for weather. All the conditions had to be right before he would agree to go.

The townspeople were also impatient, as they had kept watch on the quayside ever since the ship had been declared ready to set sail.

At last Jabez was satisfied that the weather was set fair, and the order was given to cast off. Stout hawsers that had secured the 'Jabez' to the quay were hauled away, to be coiled on the jetty until they were needed again, and slowly the ship began to move away. Captain Jabez had ordered small rowing boats to be prepared to tow her away from the land and into favourable currents, and these gently took her out into the bay. Once sure that all was well, they cast off and lay there, watching the vessel hoist sail and make out into the ocean.

On shore, the crowds sent up a cheer, and stood watching the ship get smaller and smaller, until she disappeared over the horizon. With nothing more to see they returned sadly to their homes, many of which felt empty with their masters away on the high seas.

On board, all was going well. The ship behaved beautifully. She obeyed the helm properly (seaman's way of saying she was easy to steer!) and the sails were easy to manage. On the bridge stood Captain Jabez with his hands clasped behind his back. He watched as the setting sun bathed the sky in many colours, until they were overtaken by the onset of darkness. Then the full moon rose, casting a path of light across the waters, and stars glistened in the heavens. He was utterly at peace; he was on the element he enjoyed most – the sea.

Chapter 7

THE WEATHER WAS kind to the adventurers, and the little ship ploughed steadily onwards. The weeks went by without a hitch, a steady wind blew from the right quarter so that they were able to leave the sails at a constant setting.

The crew even began to enjoy themselves. As you know, cats are not at all fond of water, and these were no exception. There was an awful lot of water around them, which at first made them very fearful. Many of them preferred to sleep curled up on the main spars, far away from the sea – and they were not frightened of heights. Most of their lives back in Merridew had been spent chasing up and down trees and, after all, masts were nothing but smoothed-down trees.

Captain Jabez, however, kept them busy. He knew the seas and their different moods; he had been through many a storm in all his days as a fisherman, and mistrusted the continual good weather. The crew were made to practice shortening sail, launching the lifeboat, and rescuing anyone who might be swept overboard. He also insisted on a clean ship, and every day details of the crew were made to scrub the decks and clean the brass, until the 'Jabez' shone like a new pin.

Boredom has always been a hazard to sailors, which taught captains to keep their men busy, and also to try to occupy their off-duty periods. On the 'Jabez', however, there was a ready-made way to spend their time.

Cats have always loved eating fish, so they did not need any persuading to get out some rods and tackle and attempt to catch them. They became quite expert, and wallowed in their favourite fresh food. There were also some competitions to see who was champion.

Sadly, though, there are always those who try to avoid any kind of work, and the 'Jabez' had its share of such creatures. Odd members of the crew could be seen creeping off into dark corners to have a snooze, and some of them were hard to catch.

Captain Catte soon put a stop to this, with the help of Sinbad, the crow, who flew patrols around the decks and rigging. Any 'skulker' who had been a bit careless in hiding himself would be rudely awoken by a prod from that wicked beak. However, the lazy ones were few and far between, and on the whole it was a very happy ship that made its way across the oceans.

Chapter 8

ONE DAY, AS Captain Jabez made his way onto the bridge, he became uneasy. He stopped in his stride and sniffed the air.

"Umph!" he grunted. "I don't like it! There's some dirty weather around somewhere!" He called out to Captain Catte, who was strolling along the main deck. "Ahoy there, Captain Catte! Could 'ee join me on the bridge, please."

Captain Catte raised his eyebrows in surprise. This was unusual. "Right away, Captain," he called out, and strode up the ladder onto the bridge, where he found Jabez staring out to sea.

"Well, Captain, what can I do for you?" he asked.

Jabez didn't take his gaze away from the horizon.

"I fear we have some trouble brewing, sir," he said. "I smells some bad weather in the offing."

Captain Catte gazed up at the clear blue sky.

"That's hard to believe," he said doubtfully. "Do you think you may be making a mistake?"

Jabez snorted with disgust.

"I've never been mistaken in all my days at sea. I smells it, I tell 'ee. Can't you feel the stillness in the air? There's trouble coming, and I don't reckon it will take too long to get here."

Captain Catte became aware of the lack of wind, and looked up to where the sails hung limply from the spars. It was a new experience for him, and he didn't much like it. Maybe Jabez was right.

"What do you think we should do, then?" asked Captain Catte.

"Well, to begin with, all sails has to be taken in and secured, then the mate and me will tour the ship to make sure there's no loose gear lying about. Every bit of cargo and equipment must be tied down tightly." He became a real action man.

"Mr Mate!" he yelled. "Muster the crew on the main deck right away – look lively!"

Impressed by the new note of urgency in the captain's voice, the mate cried, "Aye aye, sir!" and blew loudly on his whistle. He charged up and down the ship, shouting at the crew to get moving. They were not accustomed to an emergency, and didn't feel inclined to take matters seriously.

"Silly old fool!" growled one with shredded ears. "He wants to play at being captain, and I for one am not going to hurry myself." So saying, he began a leisurely stroll along the deck.

"Sinbad!" rang out a voice. "Get that man moving!" The great crow swooped joyfully upon the rebellious cat, and with a screech of pain and anger, it sped without any more delay to take its place with the other members of the crew.

Now that they were all gathered in front of him, the Captain told them of his fears. He was so convincing that they began to believe that there would be a storm, but they were not worried. They had never been in a storm at sea, so could not know what it would be like.

Captain Jabez gave his orders.

"I wants 'ee to rig up lines above the decks so that you can hold on to 'em and avoid being swept over t'side, or falling over if us rolls in the wind. Apart from those who are on watch, the rest of 'ee will stay below with the hatches battened down.

"The mate and I will check that all pumps are in working order and that the cargo is roped securely in the hold. We can't afford to lose any of our food or water."

He paused, and looked around to see what they thought of his warnings. They had listened, but had no idea what could befall them in a little while.

"'Tis all I have to say for the moment," he said. "You have work to do, and you must do it now! You've naught to fear as long as 'ee follows my orders. Get about your tasks 'til you hear the mate blow his whistle, then those of you who are not on watch, hurry down below. The rest of 'ee, take up your positions and await further orders. Good luck to you all!"

Some of the crew grinned from ear to ear, but most of them took the Captain seriously and did as they had been told. Captain Jabez, who had been studying the horizon again, caught the mate by the arm and pointed out to sea. A thin dark line of cloud stretched as far as the eye could see, and as they watched, they could see that it was moving towards them at a fair speed.

The mate blew his whistle, and the crew, who had also seen the approaching storm, hurried to do as they had been told. Suddenly it wasn't funny any longer. Those clouds looked very black, and very frightening.

"Bring 'er round to port ninety degrees, and be quick about it!" Jabez yelled to the helmsman. The ship responded immediately to the wheel. Even though all sails had been taken in, there was enough momentum on her for the turn to be made.

It was only just in time! With a frightening roar, the storm was upon them. What had at one moment been calm waters, became raging seas, with waves higher than the 'Jabez'. The vessel began to ride high on the crests, only to rush down at a terrifying speed into the troughs between the giant breakers.

All the time the wind shrieked at them, and whistled through the rigging. There was no doubt that if the sails hadn't been taken in, not only would they have been ripped apart, but the masts would have gone also. As it was, the strain was tremendous, and the masts seemed to bend before the fury.

On the bridge and on deck, those who were on duty held on with all their might to avoid being swept over the side by the water cascading over her bows. Down below, the other members of the crew huddled in fear and misery with the motion, and quite a number were feeling very ill.

Chapter 9

SUDDENLY, AMIDST THE din of the tempest, there was a loud crack, and one of the mainmasts, unable to take the strain any longer, crashed down onto the deck, only just missing those standing beneath. Captain Catte, Jabez and some of the crew grabbed axes and rushed to cut loose the mast. There was a danger in leaving it where it was, as it would make steering impossible, with one end of the mast dragging in the water.

They set to work with a will, and after many anxious moments it came free. Together, they heaved it over the side. But just as they were congratulating themselves that the danger was past, disaster fell upon them. A mighty wave caught the severed mast and sent it crashing against the side of the ship. A large hole appeared just above the water line, which in normal times would not have been a danger, but with the rolling of the 'Jabez' and the high waves, it was not long before water began to build up in the hold.

They worked frantically at the pumps, but slowly and surely the level of water rose. Heroically the crew tried to shore up the hole from inside, whilst all the time they were submerged by the sea rushing over them. It was an impossible task!

"We'll have to take to the lifeboats!" yelled Jabez above the din of the storm. "We won't be able to save her!"

He turned to the mate, "Get 'em all up from down below, and be ready to abandon ship."

The mate hastened to carry out his orders. There couldn't be much time left!

Captain Catte stood beside Jabez on the bridge, with sorrow in his heart. He thought of all the hard work that had gone into building the little vessel back in Merridew, and even he was filled with fear at the thought of taking to a lifeboat in that tremendous sea. Still, there was nothing else to be done. The ship was much lower in the water, and it was obvious that soon she must sink.

Unless they were saved by some miracle, Uncle Ebenezer's wish to study the lives of tropical fish was never to be fulfilled.

The crews were soon mustered on deck. They were a sorry-looking lot, soaked by the sea and worn out by their efforts to save their ship. Many of them collapsed from tiredness, and were past caring about the perils that awaited them. The mate drove them to their feet and bullied them into getting ready the lifeboats. Their very lives depended on it.

Captain Jabez looked across the boiling sea towards the horizon, where the light was beginning to get brighter. Sadly, he realised that the storm was nearly over, and had it not been for the mast hitting the side, the ship would have come safely through it. As they made ready to leave, the sky quickly became clearer and the waves abated.

At least, thought Jabez, they would be safe in the lifeboats and perhaps drift to land, or be picked up.

Chapter 10

SUDDENLY CAPTAIN JABEZ looked up. Something had changed!

"Don't anybody move!" he shouted. Not many were capable of moving, but those who could do so froze in their tracks, such was the command in his voice. Even Captain Catte was surprised.

"Sommat is different – can't 'ee feel it?"

Captain Catte tried to think what it was that Jabez had noticed, but he could not.

"'Tis the ship!" cried Jabez with wonder. "'Er's not sinking any more! In fact 'tis riding quite upright."

Captain Catte had to agree; it was more stable. Just then a cry rang out from some of the crew. Startled, the two captains turned to the source of the alarm. What they saw turned their hearts to stone.

Over the sides of the ship there had appeared long tentacles, and as they confronted this new horror, more and more fastened themselves onto the sides of the vessel. Fearfully, Captain Jabez leaned over the bridge rails and stared down into the sea.

"Octopuses!" he muttered. "Giant octopuses! I never seen any this big. They'll pull us down to the bottom of the ocean. We be done for sure now!"

"We must do something!" cried Captain Catte in anguish. "We can't just stand here and wait for the end." He raced along the deck and grabbed an axe. Several of the crew did the same, and they began to hack away at the giant tentacles.

But to no avail. They were so thick and strong that the blades just bounced off them. Wearily, and in despair, they gave up the struggle and sank down exhausted.

Chapter 11

BUT ANOTHER SURPRISE was in store for them! To their amazement, the 'Jabez' began to move through the water, gathering speed quite quickly. They all began to hope. Whichever way the creatures were heading, it certainly wasn't down.

Captain Catte returned to the bridge and re-joined Jabez, who could not believe what was happening. He looked over at Captain Jabez.

"Do you know what I think?" he asked with a grin.

"I wonder if it's the same thought that I've got," replied Jabez, with a half-smile.

"Well," continued Captain Catte, "I think they are here to help us. I don't know why, or where they came from. I don't know where they are taking us, and do you know what?" He paused. "I don't care. We're saved! I'm sure they can only mean to take us to safety."

With the return of hope, the crew regained their strength and good spirits. They leaned over the side and cheered the huge animals. Maybe their cheers were not heard. No matter, it made them all feel in good spirits.

For the first time since the storm had hit them, they were given a meal. In fact, because they had been so brave, the Captain ordered double rations.

On and on they went, and as they journeyed, the sea became calm and sparkled in the sunshine. Once, a school of dolphins came to visit them, leaping in and out of the waves, and playfully attacking the octopuses, who also enjoyed the sport. Out of the blue skies, gulls appeared. They wheeled around the 'Jabez', and some of them landed on the spars, where they called to the sailors in welcome.

"That's a sign we're getting near land," called Jabez to his crew. "We'll soon be able to stretch our legs ashore – I hope!" The last he said to himself, for they did not know what might be awaiting them. He shivered at the thought of providing meals for cannibals (they are natives who eat human beings!).

"Land ho!" came a cry from the bows and, sure enough, a line of surf lay ahead of them with, beyond, the shape of high mountains. Still, they were carried onwards. The land came closer and with it, the surf. The sea crashed and boiled over the line of rocks, bringing fear once again to the captains and crew.

They need not have worried, as their escorts reduced their headlong rush until the ship was moving slowly towards a break in the barrier. Safely, they passed through. Ahead of them was a stretch of smooth golden sand which came ever closer until, with a soft sigh, the 'Jabez' slid into the seabed and came to rest.

With the journey at an end, the great monsters, who had been so kind and gentle, let go their hold of the ship and swam towards the rocks. They draped themselves over the reef and settled down to a well-earned rest.

Captain Catte, although very interested in all that had been going on, stood gazing at the island, keenly taking in all the features. He turned to Captain Jabez.

"You will find this hard to believe," he said, "but I'm certain that this is one of the islands that we had intended to seek for Uncle Ebenezer's studies of tropical fish!"

Jabez was doubtful. "Are you sure? It will be a miracle if it is."

The captain gazed kindly at him. "We wanted a miracle, didn't we? And it looks as though we have one. I've been taking note of all the features I can see, and they tally with those on one of the maps. I'm sure we've made it!"

Chapter 12

CAPTAIN CATTE CALLED down to Uncle Ebenezer, who had emerged from his cabin where he had been cowering in fear. When he also had

examined what they could see of the island, he confirmed that it was indeed one of those they had intended to visit.

Captain Jabez mustered the crew together and told them the good news. Then he said: "Right-ho, men, now we know where we are, let's get the boats out and make for the shore."

However, the ship had slid so far into the sandy beach that there was no need to launch the boats. Gingerly, the crew slid down rope ladders into very shallow water and splashed ashore. We must remember that although they had become sailors – and very good ones – they were still cats, with the same fear of water. For months they had been cooped up on a ship, with nothing to see but the sea. Dangers of many kinds had beset them, including the arrival of octopuses, which at first had terrified them.

Gleefully they ran up the hard golden sands and climbed palm trees that grew nearby. Some of them had almost forgotten about trees and had got used to the masts and the rigging. Both captains stood and watched the crew enjoying themselves.

"Let's give them plenty of time to let off steam, shall we?" suggested Captain Catte. "After all, they have had little time for play all these months, and it will do them good."

Jabez readily agreed, and sat down on a large chunk of wood which lay on the beach. He pulled an old pipe and some tobacco from his pocket, and was soon puffing merrily away, warmed by the sun and free from his duties.

Captain Catte looked upon him with some affection. Jabez also deserved a rest. He had proved himself a most able captain, and without his knowledge of the sea, they would surely all have perished in the storm. Yes, he was worth his weight in gold. He joined Captain Jabez on his piece of wood.

Before long, they all decided that a meal was necessary,

so some of the crew went back on board and fetched food. A great bonfire was lit on the beach and they all had a hot picnic. After this, completely full, they settled down for cat-naps.

With the onset of evening, they collected driftwood from the shore, and lit many fires in case of unknown animals. As they had not had time to explore the island, they didn't know whether anything or anybody lived on it. It was also decided to post guards at intervals under the trees beyond the beach. That night all passed peacefully. Tiredness and full tummies made even the guards sleep!

Early the next morning, the sleepers were awakened by the sound of strange voices. They all leapt to their feet at the sight of a group of men, led by a tall, well-built man whose looks were unfortunately marred by rather ugly features. Despite this, he greeted them pleasantly.

"Welcome, my friends!" he said, approaching Captain Catte with hand outstretched. "We didn't wake you earlier, as you were all obviously very tired. We believe your ship must have been driven to our island by the storm."

"Yes," said Captain Catte. "That, and also by the wonderful help of very large octopuses. My name is Captain Horatio Catte, and these are my friends." He proceeded to introduce Captain Jabez and Uncle Ebenezer.

"I am Captain George Johnson," replied the other. "Like you, our ship was brought here several years ago. We have built ourselves a comfortable village, and we'd like you all to join us for a meal, which I am sure you can do with."

Captain Catte and all his men were delighted to accept the invitation, and followed their new friends to their village. This consisted of several one-storey buildings around a 'village green'.

A pleasant meal of cold meats and unusual vegetables was

put before them and, while eating, Captain Catte explained that this island was one of several chosen as being suitable for Uncle Ebenezer's study of tropical fish. Captain Johnson found this of great interest.

"We was amazed," said Jabez, "at how them giant octopuses saved our ship. It be a miracle they rescued us so cleverly."

"Yes, Captain," Johnson replied. "It is not generally known that octopuses are intelligent, and those in these waters are a particularly clever breed. We are very glad that they were able to bring you here to safety."

"We all decided – and rightly so – that it was a miracle!" exclaimed Captain Catte.

"Yes, that is what happened when we were shipwrecked," said Captain Johnson. "The sea creatures hovered around our vessel with curiosity. They were not unfriendly. Because our ship was something new to them, they must have decided to carry it to the shore to look it over... very lucky for us, otherwise we would have drowned. It seems that the very same happened to you!"

Chapter 13

CAPTAIN CATTE AND Captain Johnson continued their interesting chat together.

"I take it you are not married?" asked Captain Catte.

"Never had the chance," Johnson replied. "Never met a girl who liked me enough. I'm rather fierce-looking, you know, and I'm afraid they keep me at arm's length." He gazed wistfully into the distance. "Maybe one day though."

After their excellent meal, they were all taken to see the caves where the food was stored. They were huge, with great vaulted ceilings which disappeared from view into the darkness. Carcasses of meat, amongst which were many wild boars, hung on high, and lining the sides of the cavern were barrels filled with stores saved from many ships.

Captain Johnson also showed them the casks of wine which was produced on the island, grown from grapes brought in on one of the ships which had been driven to the beach. It was clear from all they had seen that the island's climate was ideal for growing practically any crop.

Uncle Ebenezer could be seen busying himself on his intended research, darting here and there, taking notes of plants and animals.

The next day, as he was walking along the beach, Uncle Ebenezer became very interested in a sea shell, and spent a long time examining it, then he wandered off along the beach.

His walk took him to the far end, where the sand ended in

a group of rocks. He watched the waves gently sweep in and break, then recede with a hiss of foam. It was restful and fascinated him.

As his gaze shifted further along, he became puzzled by a bright colour among some rocks. He made towards it until, to his shock, he found it to be a woman's dress. As he drew closer, he saw that there was indeed a woman wearing it.

Uncle Ebenezer felt rather frightened as he bent over her. He could not see how she could still be alive.

The first thing to do was to get her away from the little waves which, with the incoming tide, were creeping closer to her. Puffing and grunting with his exertions, he at last managed to get her onto the sand. To his relief he heard shouts and there, running towards him, was Captain Catte with Jabez and Captain Johnson close behind, together with several members of the crew.

The Captain knelt down by the victim and examined her, then straightened her up.

"Well, she's alive, thanks be to God. We must get her back to the village right away." He gazed down at her. "She is very young – not more than twenty, I should think – and she is very pretty."

Carefully they lifted her onto a blanket which they had brought with them, and carried her up the beach, and into the friendly warmth of Captain Johnson's home. He had insisted that she be looked after in his cottage, so that, as leaders of the island community, he could keep a fatherly watch on her.

It was obvious to the Captain that Johnson was smitten, and he could not keep back a smile as he said, "I am sure that yours is the best place for her, Mr Johnson."

Some of the ladies from the village were sent to attend to the girl, and during the next few days she began to improve.

No-one tried to find out who she was, or from whence she came, because that might have upset her. As it was, she gradually regained her strength and soon was able to sit up.

Every day Captain Johnson visited her, but kept his distance, afraid that his appearance would frighten her. One day, during one of these visits, she asked him to approach nearer, but he hung back.

"Why don't you come here where I can see you, and thank you for all your kindness," she said.

He hung his head. "I don't like to. I'm very ugly, and could frighten you."

She got up from her chair and walked slowly towards him.

"Won't you at least raise your head so that we can talk?" she asked softly. Slowly, he did as she had bid him. She gazed at him for quite a while.

"You're not at all ugly, you silly man. You have a strong face, but with a lot of kindness in your eyes. I think you are a lovely man!" She bent forward and kissed him lightly on the cheek.

He blushed bright red and, muttering something that she could not hear, ran headlong out of the room. Behind him, she smiled.

Chapter 14

OVER THE NEXT few weeks, the attraction between Captain Johnson and the girl, who told them that her name was Katie, became stronger, much to the amusement and delight of everyone.

But Captain Catte was becoming impatient. His uncle had finished collecting information concerning tropical fish in those waters, and it was generally felt that the time had come to return to Merridew.

The Captain decided that a meeting must take place, this time on the beach. As Captain Johnson was the most important person on the island, he was invited, and when Captain Catte rose to address them all, he first turned to their host.

"We are all very aware of how much we owe to you, Captain Johnson. You have shown us great kindness and hospitality, and repaired our damaged ship. We are all indebted to you. But we have been away from our homes and families for a long time and, if you are in agreement, we feel we should leave you in three days' time, which will give us time to make our preparations."

"We shall all be sad for you to go, but before you leave, I have one thing to ask of you." Captain Johnson turned to Captain Jabez.

"Sir, I have a special task for you! You are a sea captain commanding the 'Jabez', and as such you have special powers which I would ask you to exercise very shortly."

He grinned at them all and, reaching for Katie's hand, drew her to his side.

"I want you to perform the marriage ceremony for us!"

As you can imagine, the night was shattered by cheers, and Captain Johnson's hand was sore from having it shaken by everyone.

There was no point in delaying the happy event, particularly as the 'Jabez' was shortly to leave the island, so the next day the happy couple stood before Captain Jabez. It was a touching service, held on the grassy square in the centre of the village. Afterwards there was dancing, feasting, and jugs of the local wine.

At length, on the appointed day, the last farewells were exchanged and, with much waving from the ship and from the quay, the 'Jabez' slowly drew away from the quayside.

CAPTAIN CATTE
AND THE
TREASURE OF SPIDERGLASS HILL

Chapter 1

CAPTAIN CATTE HAD found an old map giving the secret of a buried treasure! And I'll tell you how it happened.

One day he had caught sight of his old enemy, Michael Mouse, scurrying along with a large piece of cheese.

"Ha!" the Captain thought. "Now's my chance to catch that little thief!" So off he went at full speed after the little mouse. But Michael, spurred on by fear, was too fast for his pursuer.

The chase was fast and furious, taking them up two flights of stairs, until they were both tearing through the large attics. The Captain was close behind, and with a squeak of relief, Michael scuttled inside the hole in a wooden wall which led to his home.

The Captain was not so lucky. Travelling at full speed, he crashed straight through the wall! There was Michael, cowering up against an old box in a dark corner, waiting for the end.

But Captain Catte was fair. He wouldn't fight a defenceless creature. He didn't know what to do next.

He became aware of the box against which Michael was crouching. It was very curious, with all sorts of carvings, and looked very old. What on earth was inside, he wondered. Treasure? He lifted the lid, and found a lot of old papers, among them was a map of a large island.

Peering closely at it, he saw an inlet with the drawing of a ship in it, and a range of mountains, in the middle of which was a clearing. Underneath was written "Spiderglass Hill".

The Captain rolled up the map and stuck it in his pocket.

"I must take this along to Uncle Ebenezer!" he muttered. "He's very clever, and he'll know what it's all about!"

By now, he had forgotten all about the little mouse, as he was so intent on calling his uncle. He was very well read, though he had a sharp tongue.

Chapter 2

UNCLE EBENEZER WAS sitting outside his cottage, in front of a small table. When his nephew arrived, he looked up.

"And what d'you want?" he snapped.

The Captain laid the map before his uncle, who peered at it intently. Then he looked up at the Captain.

"Well, I never!" he exclaimed. "You've made the discovery of the century! It's the treasure of Red Jake, the richest pirate ever to sail the Southern Seas!" He gazed up at the Captain with a satisfied smile on his face.

Captain Catte was astounded, but it was clear to him that they must go in search of the treasure – not because they wanted great wealth for themselves, but for the good it could do for Merridew County. The Captain began to pace up and down. He always did this when he was thinking.

"We must find this treasure!" he said. "But we must be careful to keep it secret, in case anyone tries to get there first! We're going to need a ship and a crew. You'll have to come with us, Uncle, as we're going to need your knowledge to find our way to the island. And we will need some of the older, more experienced fishermen, to run the ship.

"But to begin with," the Captain went on, "we must arrange for a meeting of all the cats in Merridew as soon as possible – I shall have something important to say to them!"

By means of his special messenger, Sinbad the crow, who summoned all the cats with his raucous voice as he flew,

Captain Catte ensured that all the cat population of Merridew County gathered at the huge oak tree, which was their recognised meeting place.

A great buzz of cats' talk filled the air, as they all wondered what was so important that the Captain had called them together. At a table beneath the spreading branches of the great oak tree sat the Captain and Uncle Ebenezer. Captain Catte rose to his feet, and a hush fell upon the gathering.

"Uncle Ebenezer here" – he motioned to the figure beside him – "has much to say to you." He sat down, and Uncle Ebenezer stood up.

"It is my intention," he said firmly, "to charter a sailing ship for the purpose of exploring the South Seas, and I shall need volunteers to man the ship. And you, Captain Jabez,"

he continued, addressing a stalwart cat nearby, "own an excellent ship – the 'Jabez' – which would do well for our purposes. Please will you allow us to use it?"

"Yes, certainly!" came the enthusiastic reply.

Chapter 3

NO TIME WAS wasted. No hint had been made by Captain Catte or his uncle that they were treasure-hunting, for fear that others would forestall them in their search. All preparations for provisioning the ship were made without delay. Eventually Captain Jabez was satisfied that all was ready, and gave the order for them to set sail on their journey.

The weather was kind to them, and the little ship ploughed steadily onwards. The weeks passed without a hitch and eventually they reached the island shown on the map, which Captain Catte had found in the old box.

Captain Jabez now mustered the crew and told them the true purpose of their voyage. At the mention of the word 'treasure' the crew cheered with joy and were eager to go ashore and start the treasure hunt immediately.

On shore, Captain Catte noticed a piece of wood lying on the sand. He drew Jabez's attention to it. "Look!" he cried. "There's some lettering on it. I think it's part of the name of a ship." He became very thoughtful. "This means that we're not the first vessel to fetch up on this shore."

Captain Jabez looked around him fearfully. "I wonder what became of the crew?" he said in a whisper.

"Yes, I wonder about that, too. Better not mention it to anyone else," Captain Catte advised. "It might cause a panic."

That night passed peacefully, the only noise being some rustling in the woods, which could have been the wind – but it wasn't!

Tiredness and full tummies, after their good supper, made even the guards sleep!

Chapter 4

I T WAS BROAD daylight when the first cats awoke, and what they saw made their blood curdle! They were surrounded by a line of very large creatures! The howl of the awakened cats roused the rest of the crew.

"Spiders! Huge great spiders, as big as ponies!" gasped Captain Catte. He turned to the crew. "Form a line, men! Jump to it! Let them see your claws!"

They did as they were ordered. Now the two lines faced each other; not a sound could be heard. Along the line of cats, sharp claws glistened in the sun. Suddenly, as fast as they had appeared, the huge spiders began to disappear.

"They've gone," whispered the Captain, "but they'll most likely be back, so we must be ready for them." He began to prepare their defences, marking out a portion of the beach and surrounding it with a deep trench. Into this was piled anything which would burn. Luckily there was plenty of wood lying about. At intervals, flints were placed so that the wood could be ignited.

"That should slow them down," said the Captain grimly. "But we should have a warning as to when they are coming." He placed patrols in the trees, and supplied them with whistles, so that they could alert them to the enemy's approach. "And this time, keep awake!" he snapped.

These arrangements had only just been completed when the shrill blast of a whistle came from the woods and the patrols emerged, running for the line of defences. "They're coming – hordes of them! They're very close behind us!"

They just had time to reach safety when there came the sound of a trumpet nearby! Captain Catte was amazed.

"Now where did they get that from? And who's playing it? Spiders can't play trumpets!"

As the last notes died away, hundreds – it seemed – of these huge spiders appeared on the edge of the beach and stood facing the line of defenders, who once again had shot out their claws. There was complete silence, with both sides watching each other closely.

Suddenly, a gap opened between the spiders, and the most extraordinary figure took its place between them. A spider, bigger even than any of the others, stood there. Its body was covered with a cloth of deep red material edged with gold braid; only its legs were visible. On its back was fixed a richly decorated wooden chair, also edged with gold. In fact, it was almost like a throne.

Chapter 5

I T WAS THE occupant of this chair that surprised them most – it was a man! He was not tall, but powerfully built. He had thick eyebrows and a black beard. In fact, he looked quite fearsome. A white sun-helmet protected his head, and he wore a white shirt and trousers. Altogether he was an imposing figure.

He raised a hand. "Please don't be afraid! We mean you no harm – quite the opposite. We welcome you! If there is a leader amongst you, will he come forward, so that I may meet him, and shake his hand in friendship?" He gazed at their ranks.

Captain Catte strode forward, quite an imposing figure himself, as he was in full uniform and wearing his sword.

"Well, this is an unexpected pleasure!" he said. "We hadn't thought to find any inhabitants on this island! My name is Captain Horatio Catte!"

"You're welcome here, Captain Catte! I am Sir John Bradford, and I and my crew were washed ashore several years ago, fortunately without loss of life. You reached us safely, and come in peace, I hope?"

"Yes, Sir John, and we're very glad to be here. We shall look forward to hearing all about you!" He paused. "One thing puzzles me, however. We heard the sound of a trumpeter. Who was playing it?"

Sir John laughed.

"Oh, that was Jack Jenkins, my mate! Hey, all of you, come forward and say hello to the Captain."

Sir John's crew stepped out and advanced to greet the Captain. They were all bronzed by the sun, tidily dressed, and looked very happy.

Before long, the two leaders gave orders for their men to stand down. At last they could relax and forget their fears.

"Now, I suggest we have a meal together," said Sir John,

"after which you can tell me what brought you here – if that's alright with you, of course!"

"Of course it's alright," Captain Catte assured him. "We may also ask you for your help, Sir John. We have come on a mission, but there are many things unknown to us. I have brought Uncle Ebenezer with me as he is very learned. I am sure he will also be anxious to talk to you."

"Delighted! Only too pleased to be of help, my dear fellow," beamed Sir John, patting the Captain gently on the shoulder. "But first let us eat, and I promise you a feast such as you have never had before!"

Chapter 6

THEY THOUGHT THE feast would take place on the beach, but they were wrong. Sir John insisted that they all went to his settlement. He and his men led the way to a large clearing in the woods. Here had been built a village, like Merridew, with a cluster of cottages on one side and longer, one-storey buildings on the other. In the middle was a grassed area, on which a table had been placed. Nearby, a great cauldron bubbled away next to a glowing fire, over which was a large spit. On it, some kind of meat turned round slowly, watched over by a spider, on whose head was a proper chef's hat.

Only one of his legs was needed to attend to the spit, so the others were able to prepare vegetables for the pot, which they did at great speed.

No sooner had they all begun to take this in than they were startled by a loud clanging noise splitting the air.

"Ah! The dinner gong!" beamed Sir John. "Come along now, all of you! There aren't any chairs, we never use them. Never mind, the grass is nearly always dry and it won't matter if you drop any crumbs, will it?" He laughed happily as he ushered them to the table, then placed himself between the two captains.

What a feast they had! It seemed that no sooner was a plate empty than it was filled again. At last Uncle Ebenezer sat back, nearly exhausted.

"What a meal!" he exclaimed, looking over to Sir John.

"Tell me, how on earth do you get such wonderful flavour into the vegetables? The taste is something I have never come across before. Quite, quite amazing!"

Sir John smiled at him with obvious pleasure.

"I'm very happy that you should be so pleased. We are lucky on this island. We have found many different plants in the forest which, over some years, we have tried out for cooking.

"You must put yourselves in our position. We were exploring these islands, and were caught in a storm. Our ship was wrecked. We had very little chance of being rescued, so we had to survive as best we could."

Sir John paused to collect his thoughts, then continued.

"One quite dangerous task was to collect various greens, cook them and see whether they were safe to eat. We had seen some wild animals which looked like grazing beasts, so we thought that if they can eat them, we should also be able to.

"We would cook some of these unknown plants and leave them out on the beach overnight, hoping that the creatures would eat them. They did, and as they enjoyed them and were all well afterwards, the plants were considered safe for us to eat. During this course of experimenting, we came across these delicious herbs, and that was the source of the taste which you enjoyed today." He leaned back with pride.

"Most interesting," mused Uncle Ebenezer. "If these herbs ever became known to the rest of the world, you could have a very good business. Have you ever thought of that?"

"Many times," replied Sir John. "I have always been known for having a good head for business, and naturally I can see what could be done. There is no shortage of labour, as you can see, and we could easily clear more ground for planting;

and be quite rich except for one thing: how do we get off the island? And do we really want to?

"You know, we have become very fond of the place, and we are contented with the way we live. It would need a lot of thought."

Chapter 7

UNCLE EBENEZER, BECAUSE of his wish always to improve his knowledge, questioned Sir John closely about the creatures of the island.

"I am curious to know how it is that the animals seem to do as you tell them. How on earth do you train them?"

"It's not hard to understand if you think about it," Sir John replied. "After all, I understand you, and you can talk to me although I am a human, and you are a cat. All creatures have a way of speaking; it just takes time to get to know it, just as humans from the different countries in the world learn to speak each other's languages. When we mastered their way of talking, we found it easy to teach them our ways. After all, they are very intelligent."

"Well, yes, I suppose that's true," agreed Uncle Ebenezer. "I must say, I had never thought of it that way. But what about trouble? Don't they ever fight each other, or try to eat one another?"

"They used to, before we arrived, but we were able to change the way they ate, and to grow food they could enjoy. We also get a windfall now and then." He smiled, "You are not the only visitors we have had to our island. Quite a number of ships have been driven onto our shores by storms, and most of them contain food that we cannot get here. We save as much as possible, and store it in caves not far from this clearing."

Captain Jabez, who had been sitting back half asleep after his big meal, found this interesting.

"You say a number of ships have come aground yer, yet I haven't seen any sign of their crews. What do 'ee do with 'em, and what happens to the ships?"

"There are some sailors from the ships, but they live round there," said Sir John, pointing to a distant headland. "They have made their own little town, and very nice it is. We visit them now and then and have a party, then they come here and we entertain them with a meal, much like you have had today."

"But what about the ships?" persisted Jabez.

"Ah well, that depends upon how badly they are damaged. If they can be made seaworthy again, we repair them. We have a lot of spare parts left over from the ships that cannot be put in good order. We waste nothing. It all comes into use at some time or another. Indeed, we expect you will want us to refit the 'Jabez' for you one day. I'm sure you won't want to stay with us for the rest of your lives. Of course, if any of you do want to come to live on our lovely island, you will be very welcome."

At the end of this speech, Sir John beamed at them, leant back and closed his eyes. Although he had been the perfect host, it was clear that he was tired, and Captain Catte set an example by standing up. Some of his crew, whose eyes had been getting heavier, also stood up. Sir John opened his eyes and, seeing that his guests were ready to retire, showed them to one of the larger buildings which had been made ready for them.

There was no desire to chatter, as so often happens when people go to bed, for they were all very weary after a long and tiring day. It was not long before contented snores filled the air!

Chapter 8

THE NEXT MORNING, the Captain awoke before the others, except for Jabez, who was standing in the doorway gazing out at another lovely day. As it was early and the others were still asleep, the two of them decided to take a walk.

They strolled through the forest until they reached the shore where they had landed. Jabez looked around him.

"It's gone!" he exclaimed. "The ship – it's not there!"

Captain Catte was shocked.

"We'd better get back to Sir John and tell him! This is very serious. Without the 'Jabez' we can't get home. Not unless another ship arrives, and that might not be for years!"

They ran back to the clearing, shouting for Sir John. By this time everyone was up and about. Hearing their cries, Sir John rushed to meet them, expecting news of some disaster. When Captain Catte told him the news about the ship, Sir John burst out laughing. The rest of the ship's crew stood open-mouthed with astonishment.

"My dear people," said Sir John reassuringly, "don't worry! We've taken it to our yard for some minor repairs." He took Jabez by the arm. "Come on, Captain! I will show you where it is."

With a sheepish grin, Jabez allowed himself to be led by Sir John. Everyone else followed. They crossed the beach, making towards the headland which they had seen in the distance. As they rounded the corner of the cliffs, they could hear the sounds of hammering. The closer they got, the louder became the sounds of work.

As they approached the shipyard, they were able to see what a hive of activity it was. The work party was made up entirely of spiders. The advantages were obvious. One had only to see the speed with which they covered the ground, or climbed the masts, to realise that they were just right for the job.

The ship was completely out of the water, supported by great baulks of wood, which propped it up on both sides. Sir John pointed to where a spider was repairing a small hole in the ship's side.

Jabez gazed with admiration, and chuckled at the same time. The spider had hammers in six of his hands (or whatever you call them!) whilst the other two held nails, which disappeared into the planks with great speed. Another spider was tarring the ship's bottom, whirling eight large brushes at a time. He was pulled along in a cart by two others because all his legs were in use. In that way, the job was done very quickly indeed.

Chapter 9

AFTER WATCHING FOR a while, they turned away and headed for the clearing, knowing that the stout ship 'Jabez' was in good hands – thousands of them! They were in time for lunch, which was not the great feast of the night before, but mostly fruit, with just a small amount of cold meat.

During the meal, Captain Catte asked many questions, for much still puzzled him. He wondered whether there were women and children on the island, and where they lived; he had seen none so far. It seemed that there were some, and that quite a number of families existed around the cape.

Sir John explained how many of those who were shipwrecked decided to stay on the island rather than return to their old lives, often in poverty, while many had set sail as soon as their ships were repaired.

However, by this time Captain Catte was becoming impatient. He decided that a meeting must take place on the beach. As Sir John was the most important person on the island he was of course invited, and when Captain Catte rose to address them all, he turned first to his host.

"We are all very aware of how much we owe you, Sir John. You have shown us great kindness and hospitality, but you have never asked us what made us come here."

The Captain continued: "It is only fair that you should know our purpose, and share in any benefits which might arise." He then recounted the story with its promise of treasure.

"It is now time for us to carry out the main part of our mission," said the Captain, "but only with your consent, Sir John. If you have any objections we will load up our ship and sail away back to Merridew. We will never tell anyone else of our map, so you may continue to live in peace."

Sir John rose to his feet.

"My very dear friends," he began, "I am amazed to hear this story, and I cannot rest until I have helped you in your treasure hunt." He grinned. "Oh yes! I'm coming with you. Wild horses wouldn't keep me away! I have always liked adventure, and this is the first real chance of some excitement since we came to live here.

"As far as a share is concerned, I have some ideas on that already, but first let's find the treasure!"

Chapter 10

BY THE TIME the meeting broke up, it had been decided to set off inland in three days. Time was needed to get stores together, set out a route, etc., and work out the order of march. It was pretty obvious that there would be some very rough country ahead of them – the distant mountains and hills made sure of that. In addition, the vegetation would be thick, with very few ways through it. *Some task!* thought the Captain.

At last, the day arrived for their trek into the undergrowth. Piles of stores lay on the beach, and all the adventurers were assembled. Captain Jabez had been given the task of arranging which load every man (or cat) should carry. It looked heavy! The journey was going to be long and tiring!

Presently, from the trees came Sir John and his party. They all looked very cheerful.

"What have they got to be so cheerful about?" grumbled one grizzly old tom. "Just wait 'til they see what they've got to carry!"

"Good morning! Good morning!" boomed Sir John. "We certainly have a lovely day to start our journey. I've been so excited that I haven't had a wink of sleep!" He gazed around him at the piles of stores. "My word, there surely is a mountain of stuff here! Have we got to take it all with us?"

"'Fraid so," said Jabez. "Us don't know how long it'll take us to reach Spiderglass Hill, so us needs plenty of reserves. There be medicines and bandages, and Uncle Ebenezer's specimen bottles for collecting wild flowers and so on. 'Fraid everyone's going to have quite a load to carry."

Sir John stared in disbelief. "Did you say carry? Do you really think that a load like this can be carried over the rivers and the mountains of the jungle?"

He paused and looked at Captain Catte for an answer. For once, the Captain was unsure of himself. He had to admit that he saw no other way of doing it.

"We have no alternative," he said. "I wish we had. None of us wants this burden, but then we do need all this equipment."

He waved at the cases which lay before him. "If you can suggest a better way, I'm sure we'll all be very grateful to you."

"I'll do better than that." Sir John turned to his mate, Jenkins, who was standing beside him. "Jack! Sound the call on your trumpet!"

Jack Jenkins lifted the instrument to his lips, puffed out his cheeks and blew.

The stirring notes rang out for all to hear. After a short interval, from amongst the trees emerged a line of spiders. Sir John had obviously planned this, for each spider had a railed platform on its back, with a little seat in the front.

Sir John laughed with delight at the look on all their faces.

"Just a little surprise for you, my friends! This should make our task a lot easier, don't you think? To tell you the truth I'm a very lazy man, and I was just as anxious as you were when I saw what had to be taken with us. Now, load up and hop aboard, then let's get going!"

So, with cries of glee, they climbed on the backs of the good old spiders, the packages were loaded behind them and, led by Sir John, they began their journey to Spiderglass Hill.

Chapter 11

I T WAS SENSIBLE for someone from the island to lead them as, once among the trees, there was no sight of the hills or any of the landmarks that they had come to know. At first the trail led through gentle forests and streams, making progress easy, but soon this gave way to more rugged ground. Sir John reached the limit of his knowledge and handed over the lead to Captain Catte. Beside him rode Jabez, because with his skill of navigation their route would be easier to plot.

The thicker the jungle became, so the cats' ability to see in the dark showed its usefulness. They were able to guide their mounts so that obstacles such as tree trunks and rocks were avoided.

After two days of tramping through tangled forest, they emerged into more open country, with the mountain range rising clearly in the distance. In front of them flowed a wide river, with its clear water sparkling in the sunlight. Here, Captain Catte called a halt.

He stood up on his spider's platform and raised his voice so that all could hear him.

"Here, with the help of our good spiders and the rest of you, we have made excellent progress, but I expect you are all as tired as I am. I therefore propose that we make camp beside the river and rest for a day." A great sigh of relief went up from the company and they began to dismount.

"Just a minute! I have more to say!"

They stopped talking and turned to listen to him.

"We will make this our base camp and unload most of the stores. We are not far from our goal now, and it won't need all of us for the final stage. I will select a smaller party for this, and the rest of you will be kept here in reserve. We don't know what may await us in the mountains."

There was a murmur of assent from the listeners, and the Captain continued, "Captain Jabez will be with me, to help me find the way, and Uncle Ebenezer will want to see what he can find for his research, so he has to come."

Chapter 12

THE COMPANY IMMEDIATELY set about the task of preparing the camp. The weather was fair and there was no need for tents, but food had to be cooked, so fires had to be started and the provisions set out. Precautions also had to be taken to guard against any nasty surprise, for although the island was a peaceable place, this area was unknown and there could be dangers.

When all was ready, the cats and their friends sat down to a satisfying meal, for standards had to be kept up wherever they were. The spiders looked after their own diet, which was mostly made up of tasty grubs. Soon after, with fires glowing around the camp, and guards posted, the air became filled with the sound of heavy snores!

The next day dawned fine and clear. Nothing horrible awaited the awakening adventurers, and no nasty dreams had disturbed their slumber. The thought of the journey that they were to undertake that day filled the special party with excitement – and some nervousness!

After they had eaten an early breakfast, the loads were again packed onto the backs of the spiders and, with their passengers also aboard, they set about crossing the river.

Now here the Captain had another surprise! He did not know that the spiders could swim, but these large ones could – and did, with great speed. Because of all their legs and the lightness of their bodies – even with their loads – they swam across the river in double-quick time.

Soon the party was heading out across the plain towards the mountains. Even though the spiders travelled quickly, it was not until late morning that they once again came to the edge of a forest. It was decided upon that a good hour's rest and some food should be taken as it was likely to be the last opportunity they would have for some time.

Eventually they were ready to leave, so after making sure that their camp site was left clean and tidy, they went on their way. The trees were not so dense, but the going was hard, with huge rocks and steep cliffs to climb. They were in the mountains now, and it was the most difficult part of their journey.

It was now that they were made to value the ability of the spiders. Their long legs soon made short work of these hardships, and they made good progress. As the spiders covered the ground, they wove webs which stretched out behind them. Captain Jabez couldn't see the point of it.

"Stupid, I calls it!" he said. "What's the point of doing that now? We're past the parts where they were necessary. Better if they'd done it before we got here."

Sir John turned to him and said, not unkindly, "It's for the journey back. You see, they have worked it out that there might be more to carry, and they're already laden down with us and our baggage. They're very intelligent."

Captain Jabez looked a bit crestfallen, and mumbled to himself.

Suddenly they came to a halt. They were at the top of a mighty cliff, and below them – a very long way down – was a valley. In the middle of this valley was a steep hill, with a peculiar rock lying on the top of it.

Captain Catte turned to Uncle Ebenezer in awe.

"We've made it, Uncle! It's the end of our search – that's Spiderglass Hill! I recognise it from the old map!"

Ebenezer confirmed that it was so, and they made preparations to reach the bottom of the cliff.

"Everyone stay on the spiders!" shouted Sir John. "And hold on very tightly! I advise any one of you who are scared of heights to close your eyes." He led the way, and really it was quite a good sport, because the spiders let themselves and their passengers down on more webs. The more adventurous members of the party enjoyed it immensely, and were sorry when it was all over.

Eventually they were all standing on the plain, looking up at the needle-like hill with the curious rock perched on top.

"Hmm, don't much like the look of that!" said Sir John, peering up at it anxiously. "It might tumble down at any moment and squash us!"

"No chance of that!" Uncle Ebenezer assured him. "It's quite safe. I've seen this kind of thing before, and read about it." He broke off and stared up at the rock. Something was happening!

Chapter 13

ON TOP OF the rock were two holes which looked just like eyes, and these were beginning to glow. As they watched, the light became stronger and stronger, until it hurt to look!

"Now, see what happens to that light!" Despite the glare, Ebenezer was keeping his gaze steadily on it. "It's nearly midday, and I reckon that will be the time when we have the answer to our quest." He was right. At the exact hour of twelve, two beams of light shot out from the 'eyes' and met.

"Quick – mark that spot!" commanded Ebenezer. "Hurry, or you'll be too late!"

"Look lively, you loafers!" Captain Jabez had also joined in. Some of the crew ran to the spot and planted a thick rod where the beams met.

"Break out the shovels! What are you waiting for?" Even Captain Catte was affected by the urgency, and he was one of the first to start digging.

They kept at it for a long time. Deeper and deeper they went but nothing came to light. Some of the party began to moan and blame Ebenezer.

"Silly old fool! I expect he's got it all wrong. Going mad just because of the sun's rays. Probably got a touch of the sun himself!"

One of the crew threw down his spade with disgust. It bounced off the side of the large hole they had dug, and dislodged a great wedge of earth. As it slid down, a wooden doorway was revealed!

They gasped with surprise.

"Well, your bad temper has been of good service to us," grinned the Captain. "I suppose someone had better get it open, and then we'll see what lies within." There was no mad rush; indeed, everyone seemed a little in awe of that rather sinister door which had remained hidden for all those years.

Eventually, Uncle Ebenezer moved towards it. He reached the door and caught hold of a tarnished brass handle. He pushed and pulled with all his might, but it would not open. Captain Catte tried, Jabez tried, in fact they all tried, but it was no use. It would not shift.

Tired from their exertions, they sat around and discussed their next move. Uncle Ebenezer sat apart from them, concentrating his mind on the problem. Presently he leapt to his feet.

"Aha!" he cried, "I have it! Here, nephew, come with me!" Taking Captain Catte by the arm, he led the way down into the hole and up to the door. "Catch hold of the handle and push it sideways – not the handle, you idiot – the door – I think it slides open!"

Captain Catte bent to the task, but it still didn't want to open. Just as Ebenezer was beginning to doubt himself...

"It's shifting!" gasped the Captain. "I felt it move. Come on, some of you, lend me a hand!"

Suddenly it gave way, causing all those working on it to fall in a heap.

"Don't just lie about!" snapped Ebenezer. "There's work to be done. First of all we must have some light. Come on, come on!"

There were no such things as electric torches in those days. People made use of thick pieces of wood, tarred on the end. These were ignited with a flint, and carried in the hand.

Peering into the cave, what they saw made them gasp in wonderment. A large room had been carved out of the rock, and it was filled with wooden chests. Filled with excitement, Sir John and Captain Catte opened them, to find that they were filled with golden coins and precious-stoned ornaments. Stacked against the walls were larger gold articles such as candlesticks and vases of every shape and size.

To their horror, amongst all this treasure lay two skeletons, dressed in seamen's clothing, which grinned at them from empty skulls.

"Just what I expected to find," observed Ebenezer. "They must have been the two men who probably dug out this secret room and carried all this treasure in here. That pirate Red Jake could not let them live – they might have told someone about it, or even killed Red Jake and kept the treasure for themselves. So he got rid of them."

With this gruesome information in the forefront of their minds, they all set to with a will, clearing the cave of its treasure. They were in a hurry to leave the spot and return to the more peaceful atmosphere of Sir John's village.

Even with this to spur their efforts, it was dark when it was all completed, so they decided to make camp for the night. None of them could sleep very well – many dreamed of being chased by skeletons! It was with relief that they saw the sun rise, and with it the start of their journey home.

Chapter 14

THEY WERE NOW very grateful for the webbed ropes spun by the spiders on the way to Spiderglass Hill. As they had foreseen, there was much more to be carried than before, which meant that the spiders had to use most of their legs for that purpose. This they were able to do by using the support of their webs and their free legs. Because of this, the way back to the base camp did not prove too difficult.

Before long they were at the riverside, where they met the main party which had crossed to assist them. When they saw the treasure which had been found, they were amazed and overjoyed. Their expedition had been a complete success!

Their trek back held no dangers or problems, so it was with joy that they were received by the villagers later the next day. The procession was headed by Jack Jenkins, who blew his trumpet so lustily that it seemed his cheeks would burst.

That night there was another feast, equally as good as the first they had been given, and it went on into the early hours of the morning. It was all very jolly, with everyone sitting around the long tables which groaned under the weight of the delicious food. Everything glowed in the light of the many torches among the trees.

Afterwards there was dancing, and much drinking of jugs of local wine. Captain Catte was heard to groan, "You know, much more of this feasting and I shall be as fat as those pigs in the forest!"

Uncle Ebenezer had heard his remark.

"I know what you mean, nephew. I think it's time we went home. Even I am missing Merridew County."

"My own thoughts," agreed the Captain. "I will have a talk with Sir John and see about the ship being prepared for sailing. There are also other matters."

He talked to the other members of his party, and found that they were also yearning for Merridew. After all, they had been away for a very long time.

So, the next day he sat down with Sir John and told him of their decision. Sir John looked very serious – and sad.

"I understand perfectly, Captain. I'm sure I would feel the same. I will have the ship brought round in a day or two, and filled with stores and water, and of course"... he smiled, "the treasure."

"Now that's something I want to discuss with you," broke in Captain Catte. "We think you should share it equally with us. After all, we would never have found it if it hadn't been for you!"

Sir John smiled once again.

"What would we do with the treasure? What would we spend it on? No, I have an idea to put to you. Do you remember talking to me about the special herbs and spices we use?" The Captain nodded. "Well, how would it suit you to put some of the proceeds of the treasure to starting a trade between our two countries? We would clear more land and increase our crops, and you could provide transport and a market for use in Merridew and beyond."

Uncle Ebenezer, who had been in on the discussion, was full of enthusiasm.

"A capital idea, my dear Sir John, and one which would

benefit us all – not only in trade, but in giving us the opportunity to see each other again." He had come to like Sir John very much indeed.

That was the end of the discussion, as all parties were thrilled with the plan.

A week later saw the 'Jabez' riding by the quay, with her crew lining the decks. The whole of the island's population was there to see them off. The anchor was weighed, some sails hoisted, and gradually they drew away from the quayside. The crowd continued to wave, even when the 'Jabez' was a mere speck on the horizon. On board, everyone was quiet, the only words spoken being the commands needed to run the ship. They were going home, but leaving many friends behind.

Chapter 15

MERRIDEW COUNTY HAD been like a ghost town since the explorers had set sail. Most of the menfolk had gone, leaving only the old and infirm. The women went about their tasks without much enthusiasm, and as time went on they began to be afraid. They wondered whether they would ever see their loved ones again.

One morning, which began very much like all the others, a cry went up from the few who were about.

"Look at the beacon – it's been lit!"

Now this was a sign that a strange ship was approaching! The rest of the inhabitants came to their doors, then they all rushed down to the harbour to see for themselves. Sure enough, just over the crest of the horizon was a sailing ship. As it came nearer, the sharper-eyed shouted in joy.

"It's the 'Jabez'! They're coming home!"

Hurriedly, they made preparations for a celebration. Somehow a few bandsmen were assembled. The moment they had all been waiting for was here!

The women ran to put on their best clothes, and all the children were scrubbed clean. Bunting festooned every building and, of course, the sun shone out in welcome.

Up on the deck of the 'Jabez', excited members of the crew lined the sides, waving to the cheering crowd.

Then came the orders for which they had been waiting.

"Take in all sails!" bawled Jabez. "Prepare to receive mooring lines." Then before long, "All members of the crew may now go ashore!"

He grinned at Captain Catte, who stood beside him on the bridge.

"Well, sir – we made it! And what a grand welcome they have given us!"

Captain Catte shook his hand.

"You have performed your duties with great gallantry and bravery. With your help, our expedition in search of the buried treasure has been a complete success!"

CAPTAIN CATTE
AND THE
BOUNCERS

Chapter 1

CAPTAIN CATTE WAS bored!

He sat in his favourite chair, looking very grumpy. The trouble was that in the past he had been involved in many schemes and adventures, and now he was missing them! He craved excitement.

With a deep sigh he rose up, put on a battered old military coat and hat, and left the house. He made his way down the main street, at the bottom of which, near to the harbour, lived his Uncle Ebenezer, who was very clever and wise. He owned many books, and read most of the time – that is, when he was not collecting information about tropical fish, and flowers from many foreign lands.

He was poring over an ancient book when Captain Catte arrived and greeted him. His uncle grunted and then said, "What have you come for, nephew? Can't you see I'm busy? There's such a lot I still don't know about tropical plants, and books don't tell me everything. I'd like to go on another trip, like the one we did when I wanted to study tropical fish on that island off the coast of Africa."

The old cat looked up at the Captain. "What about going to another of the African islands, so that I can search for my flowers?"

"That's just what would suit me!" exclaimed his nephew. "I've been feeling bored stiff, and a good sea voyage would cheer me up!"

So off he went to talk it over with his wife, Mrs Jones, and with his good friend Captain Jabez. Both were enthusiastic over the idea, and Jabez put his stout ship – the 'Jabez', named after him – and his trusty crew, at the disposal of Captain Catte and his uncle.

Mrs Jones had some very firm ideas about this expedition. After telling her all about it, the Captain continued, "You don't mind, do you? Even if it means danger, and for me to be away from home for a long time?"

"Mind, Horatio?" she quipped. "Of course I mind, and this time I'm coming with you. There'll be no argument about that!"

The Captain was about to open his mouth to protest, but seeing Mrs Jones with her hands on her hips and legs slightly apart, he decided that now was not quite the right time to argue with her.

"She could always change her mind at a later date," he thought. At this moment, though, it would be just as well to agree with her.

"Of course you can come, my dear!" he said. "I'm glad you suggested it, because I for one will be pleased to have you aboard!"

Chapter 2

PLANS NOW HAD to be made with the assistance of Captain Jabez, by means of a meeting at the ancient 'meeting tree'. Word was quickly sent with the help of his tried and trusted assistant, the crow known as Sinbad, and soon Captain Catte and Jabez stood before a large crowd of assembled cats, many of whom had been on previous adventures with him.

Captain Catte called for silence, and in a loud commanding voice he cried, "It has come to my attention that many of you cats present are suffering from boredom." He paused, waiting for the words to sink in, and then continued. "I have become very bored of late, and I would like to have a show of hands from those of you who are also bored."

He gazed at each cat in turn, and slowly all the cats raised their hands. What he saw before him resembled a forest of waving hands, and he smiled to himself.

Clearing his throat, he continued, "Well then, I may be able to help at least some of you to overcome your boredom."

The cats pressed closer to hear him.

"I have been talking to Uncle Ebenezer. As you know, he is very interested in tropical plants, and he has asked me if I will take him to explore one of the islands off Africa, to search for rare plants, and Captain Jabez here has agreed to take us there in his ship, the 'Jabez'. We shall want those of you who have been with him before to act again as his crew. Are you willing to do this?"

There came an enthusiastic roar from those cats who had travelled as crew on the 'Jabez' on previous adventures with Captain Catte and Jabez.

"Right!" said the Captain, "We will make preparations to sail as soon as possible, and who knows whether once more we may have some exciting adventures!" Little did Captain Catte know what was before them!

Chapter 3

THE VOYAGE OF the 'Jabez' was bound to be a long one. There were many days to be spent at sea, and Captain Jabez made sure that all the crew were kept fit and busy. Boredom, through not having enough to do, only leads to mischief. On the Captain's orders, races were held up and down the masts and rigging. This kept the crew agile. Sails were taken in and re-set, boats were lowered and taken back on board for practice. The whole crew took turns in manning the lifeboats, and as a result, became first rate oarsmen.

Thanks to all these activities, the time passed quickly. The crew also had the interest of watching the various sea creatures which came to have a look at them. Porpoises and dolphins were regular visitors, frolicking in the sea just clear of the 'Jabez'.

Mrs Jones, who had decided to accompany them, was finding it very quiet. She was used to having the grandchildren around her, and to calling on the neighbours to catch up on village gossip. But she never complained, and the Captain secretly admired her for not doing so. In his heart he was very pleased that she hadn't changed her mind. It was good company he needed at the end of a long day, and besides, her cooking was splendid!

She often appeared on deck, contentedly doing her knitting. One day she raised her head and sniffed the air. She put down her work.

"I think we're getting near some land," she said, "I can smell trees!" She was right! Captain Jabez pointed ahead, where a dark line could be seen on the horizon. A great cheer went up from the cats. The journey across the ocean had been long, and besides, they had been surrounded by water, and cats don't really like it! They all hoped for a quick return to dry land.

The 'Jabez' slowly drew near to the land, and Jabez carefully looked out for a suitable bay where the ship could be docked. Eventually he gave the order for the anchor to be dropped in a sheltered cove.

Here, Captain Catte came into his own again as organiser. He sent out patrols to find a suitable site for their camp, and before long one of them returned, with the good news that they had found a grassy clearing in the forest, and a stream running through it. But there had been no sign of any creatures or inhabitants.

Jabez then sent word back to the ship that the crew was to join them, with the exception of a group to stay on guard.

The crew were immediately ordered to build a camp, while Mrs Jones took on the organising of the cooking, and sent out a party to catch some fish.

"And don't you eat it all before you get back!" she warned them, knowing the appetite cats have for fish!

At this point, the last patrol returned, saying that they had seen animals that looked like goats up the mountain slope. Captain Catte was delighted to hear this, as goats meant milk – something that cats loved and had not had since they left Merridew.

Chapter 4

CAPTAIN CATTE AWOKE to the songs of the birds, and the warming rays of the rising sun. Mrs Jones asked, "What's the plan for today?"

"I intend to take a party up onto the mountain," he replied.

"It would be good if we could capture some of those goats for their milk. And I know that Uncle Ebenezer will want to start his search for the rare flowers he's hoping to find here. What will you do whilst I'm away, my dear?"

She drew herself up, and said firmly, "I intend to come with you, husband!"

He knew that he was on dangerous ground when she called him 'husband'. She had made up her mind and could be very stubborn.

"Do you think that's wise?" he asked warily. "We don't know what to expect. There may be animals, swamps, snakes. Don't you think it's a job for us men?"

"I certainly do not!" she said firmly. "I've made up my mind."

She bustled off, but over her shoulder said, "I'm just going to get a few things ready for the journey," – then she was gone.

The Captain sighed. "Oh well," he said to himself, "better make the best of it." He sat down and waited for her to return, which wasn't long. She was carrying a large bag.

"What on earth have you got there?" he asked in astonishment.

"Why, my knitting, of course."

"Your knitting?" He couldn't believe it. "What are you going to make then, a jumper in case it gets cold?" His voice was heavy with sarcasm.

"How witty of you, Catte! You should share your wit with the others. I'm sure they'd benefit from it!" He bit his lip, for she could be really nasty sometimes.

"Very well, my dear," he said. "I expect you know best."

"I usually do," she smirked, then said briskly, "Come on,

let's get going. We've wasted too much time already with all your talk."

By now, he was completely subdued, and led his men and his wife into the forest. He reflected on how much easier it was to handle the men on the ship than Mrs Jones!

Amongst the trees it was dark and cool, a welcome change from the heat of the clearing. They tramped past acres of beautiful wild flowers, bright with many colours and with delightful scents. Bees worked among the blossoms – not small bees like they knew at home, but ones much larger. One of the crew, in high spirits, playfully swiped at one of the bees, only to let out a yell of pain.

"Serves you right!" laughed one of his mates. "That'll teach you to be more careful!"

It was a long march. Now and then they caught a glimpse of the volcano through a break in the foliage. The thought of goats and fresh milk spurred them on, although by now they were very weary.

Chapter 5

BEFORE LONG, THEY were in the middle of the forest, and it was much darker. There was something sinister about the place, and nobody sang or talked.

Suddenly, Captain Catte reeled back in alarm, letting out a cry of fear. From above, a great long serpent swung down in front of him!

"A snake, look out!" he yelled. But they had all seen it and started back in terror, falling over each other in a bid to escape.

"Oh, I say!" the serpent spoke, in a very cultured voice. "Please don't be afraid. I only want to say 'How do'. I don't mean you any harm, and I'm not a snake, you know!"

Recovering from this latest shock, the Captain was able to take a closer look at the creature. He had to grin! On its head it wore a sailor's cap, then the face! – two large eyes, a large mouth split wide with a smile, a tiny nose... and a nicely trimmed moustache! How could he have any fear?

He bowed low. "Captain Horatio Catte at your service, sir."

The creature inclined its head. "Charmed, I'm sure. My name is Cecil. I took the name from some papers I found. Suits me, don't you think?"

Captain Catte agreed. Everyone had now forgotten to be afraid and were keen to know more about Cecil. It was Mrs Jones who asked the first question.

"You certainly look like a snake, even if you say you are not," she said. "What are you?"

"First, dear lady, I must tell you that I am not the only one. Oh heavens, no! There are lots of us. It just so happens that I was chosen to come and look you up. It was my turn, you see."

Jabez chimed in. "What are you then, and where do 'ee all live?"

Cecil had been looking at them; he was puzzled.

"Excuse me, old chap, but I'm curious about you. I've never seen anything like you before."

"Oh, we're cats," answered Jabez, "and there be lots of us too!"

"That's a peculiar name – cats! I must remember that. But how rude of me! You asked me where we live. Why, in the volcano, of course!"

Captain Catte found this extraordinary. "But what about the danger?" he asked. "Suppose it erupted – you'd all be killed."

Cecil was surprised. "Why on earth should it do that? It's been quiet for as long as anyone can remember."

Captain Catte persisted. "But it looks perilous. We saw smoke coming from it. That must mean it's still active."

Cecil looked up at the volcano and smiled.

"You needn't worry about that! The smoke is from our cooking stoves, and that reminds me, I'm feeling a trifle famished. I say, why don't you all join us for dinner? There's always too much." He glanced at their dusty clothes. "We are quite informal, you know," he said hurriedly, grinning at them in good humour. "Please say yes, it would be such fun."

Chapter 6

THEY WERE ALL eager to accept his offer, except Mrs Jones.

"Aren't you forgetting something?" she asked, addressing Cecil.

He looked puzzled. "Am I? What on earth can that be?"

"I asked you a question," Mrs Jones reminded him, "and I'm still waiting for an answer. What are you?"

Cecil gazed down at her kindly. "I am truly sorry, madam. You did ask me, and with shockingly bad manners, I forgot to tell you." He paused, then said slowly, "We are the rubber people." He held up his hand as they all began to talk at once.

"Let me explain," he said. "Our bodies are different to yours. Our bones, muscles, and so on have the ability to stretch, just like rubber. As you can see, we can change our shape. To take on the properties of a snake was not to frighten you. It was the simplest way of getting close. After all," he finished, with a grin, "you didn't look upwards very often, did you? Just you watch this."

With a few twists and grunts, his whole appearance changed, and he became just like a human being, although a rather plump one.

"See?" he said.

They much preferred his new shape, and, with light hearts, they followed as he led them towards his settlement. For Uncle Ebenezer's benefit, he pointed out the rare and beautiful plants to them, and gave them their names. Mrs

Jones was also very interested, as she loved gardening. With all her doubts about him having disappeared, she walked beside Cecil, listening as he explained everything to her.

It was a fair distance, and Mrs Jones began to tire. Cecil was concerned.

"Here, let me assist you, dear lady," he said. With this, his legs disappeared, and now he resembled a large rubber ball with arms. He made a dent in his back.

"Climb up and just relax," he said. Gingerly she obeyed. It was quite comfortable, and soon they were gently bouncing along the path.

"I'm quite talented, don't you think?" he asked Mrs Jones. The Captain watched this with some amusement. His wife and Cecil were becoming good friends, with Cecil doing his best to answer her many questions.

They learnt that the rubber people had known no other place than the island. They were very happy, they had everything they needed for a comfortable life. They mostly ate fish and fruit. However, there was a particular tree which they called the 'meat tree', because the seeds tasted like meat.

"How on earth do 'ee know what meat tastes like?" asked Jabez.

"Oh, there's no mystery about that," replied Cecil. "You see, there were other visitors to our island before you. One party even brought casks of provisions with them. They obviously had decided to form a settlement. I soon put a stop to that, though!" he smirked. "They were so frightened by my snake form that they fled back to their ship, leaving everything behind. Amongst other things was meat – sausages, I believe they called it. Well, we tried it all and liked it. Then we found the tree.

"In passing, let me put your mind at rest. The rubber

people do not go around naked." Indeed, when he had stopped being a snake, Cecil had reached into a hollow in a tree, and taken from it a garment. It was rather like an old-fashioned swimming costume, being striped and having short sleeves and short legs. If a rubber person changed shape, the garment did also, as it was made of a kind of elastic material.

Chapter 7

AS SOON AS he heard that others had also landed on the island, the Captain's interest was aroused. He questioned Cecil about them.

"Tell me, Cecil, do you know what they did when you turned them away?"

Cecil thought for a moment. "I believe they made for the mainland. There is certainly someone living there. We see their ships on occasions."

"You're sure they went to the mainland?" asked the Captain. "It's vital that we're sure."

"My dear Captain," Cecil replied, "I can point out to you where I think they are. We see most things from our volcano. Their ship puts into the bay just around the point." He shook with mirth. "They won't come here again, though – they might encounter a fierce serpent!"

Whilst they had been talking, they moved up a gentle slope leading towards the volcano. They now began to climb. The going was much more difficult, as underfoot it was thick dust, and the path proceeded in a zigzag. They were beginning to tire, and they wondered whether the goats and the promise of milk would be worth all the hard slog!

At last, they reached the summit. What they saw astounded them. A gentle slope led down to a large and lush valley, where goats grazed peacefully. The patrol had not been wrong. Cecil led them down into the valley. Tiny cottages nestled in fruit orchards. Smoke from chimneys showed that cooking was taking place. Some of the dwellings were quite large, and were obviously occupied by families.

It was just like a village back home, thought Mrs Jones. She was determined to talk to some of the villagers soon. By this time, she had decided to walk, as Cecil seemed to be tiring.

"It's a beautiful place, isn't it?" Captain Catte asked her. "Have you looked at the people? They're very much like the humans back home, only rounder."

Mrs Jones agreed. She had been thinking the same thing, and was itching to get closer to them. She was not kept waiting for long. The inhabitants were just as curious as the cats! They crowded round the party, talking amongst themselves, the boldest even reaching out to touch them.

Cecil led them on down into the valley, and eventually they came to a very large house. Cecil stopped outside.

Chapter 8

"WELL, HERE WE are!" said Cecil, waving a hand towards the house. "This is where I live." They gazed at it in wonderment. *He must be a most important person,* thought Jabez.

"Before we enter," said their host, "I don't think you should call us rubber men. It's such a mouthful! Just call us Bouncers – we'll be very happy with that." He grinned at them and moved towards a most imposing door.

"Come on, follow me!" he cried.

They moved forward, and the door ahead of them was opened by an ageing, bent old chap with a fringe of white hair around a large bald head. He wore dark breeches and a striped coat.

"My butler," whispered Cecil.

The old gentleman inclined his head. "Welcome home, sir," he intoned solemnly.

"Thank you, Boris, most kind. By the way, these good people are to be my guests. Would you ask Cook to very kindly arrange a meal for us all?"

"Indeed, sir, arrangements have already been made. We heard about the ship's arrival, then saw you leading the way towards us, so I took the liberty of issuing some instructions."

"Well done indeed, Boris!" exclaimed Cecil. "What a treasure." He turned to the company. "Without Boris, the whole place would go to the dogs!"

Boris was not put out by his flattery.

"I do what I consider to be my duty, sir. I take pleasure in serving you." With this, he bowed to them and, with great dignity, made his way to his own little room, the butler's pantry.

Cecil turned to his guests. "If you feel anything like me, you must be longing for a rest and clean up. I'm going to my rooms to make myself ready for dinner, and I'm sure you would all like to do the same thing. We've plenty of bedrooms and bathrooms, so I'll just get someone to sort you out with what you need."

Cecil rang a bell and in a short while it was answered by a jolly little lady with pink cheeks. Cheerfully she led them to a wide stairway onto the first floor. She opened a door to reveal a long room with two rows of very comfortable beds. The cats purred with delight, but there was more to see. She showed them through another door leading off the dormitory. They gasped with amazement, some of them with horror!

Nearly all the space was occupied by a huge bath, and above it was a shower big enough to reach every corner. Cats don't like water, but such was their condition that most of them could hardly wait to get into it.

Mrs Jones, however, was not happy. She did not fancy sharing a bath with the rest of them. The maid could see that she was troubled. Putting a hand on Mrs Jones' arm, she reassured her.

"Now, you are not to worry! I've been told to give you and the Captain your own little suite. Just you follow me!"

They followed her up the corridor where she showed them into a most luxurious apartment. It was deeply carpeted, and there was a three piece suite that invited one to sit in it. Between the chairs was a highly-polished table on which had been placed a vase of gorgeous flowers.

And the bed! It was quite the biggest in the world! It was a four-poster, with a canopy of pink silk, which matched the bed cover. To complete the picture, two snow-white pillows awaited tired heads.

They were both overcome, but the maid hadn't finished with them! She showed them another door leading off from the bedroom.

"That's your bathroom," she said. "You'll find all the usual things there."

So saying, she bustled off about her other chores. When they had recovered from all these pleasant shocks, they decided it was time to begin their clean-up programme. Mrs Jones was first in the bathroom, whilst the Captain, like every wise commander, went to see the crew. The door was opened by a very clean Jabez. His face was wreathed in a happy smile.

"'Pon my word, sir, us 'av come to the right berth this time!" He beckoned the Captain to enter. "Here, take a look at all this!"

Lying on the beds were about half the crew, all sparkling clean.

Making their way to the bathroom, they first noticed the noise, then they saw what was causing it. The cats were splashing each other, and shrieking with the fun of it all. The Captain looked on in envy.

"Oh, what it is to be young," he sighed.

After a while, he left them to their games and went back to his own quarters. Mrs Jones was fast asleep, so he tiptoed to the bathroom and had a quick wash and brush up. Then he eased himself gently down onto the bed beside her and soon he too sank into oblivion.

After some time, there came a knock on the door.

"Who is it?" called the Captain, a trace of irritation in his voice.

"'Tis Jabez, sir. I had a notion you were still asleep, so I thought I'd better tell you. They're ringing the dinner gong."

The Captain woke Mrs Jones, and they both found that they were very hungry indeed. They made their way down the wide staircase, to find Cecil waiting for them.

Chapter 9

"WELCOME BACK!" HE laughed, and took them into a sumptuous room. The rest of the crew were already there. Cecil ushered them both into comfortable chairs.

"Now, I know that you're all longing to eat, and so am I, but we must first have a drink."

He rang a bell, and Boris appeared, holding aloft a silver tray, upon which were glasses filled with amber liquid. Other members of the staff followed him, also carrying trays. Soon everyone had a glass. Cecil raised his.

"To my very welcome guests, who are also my friends!" They joined him in tasting their drinks. It was magnificent! None of them had tasted anything like it. Captain Catte was very impressed.

"My word, this is wonderful!" he exclaimed. "Where on earth did it come from?"

"Not on earth really, old fellow," replied Cecil. "You see, the water that we use to manufacture it comes from inside the volcano, so it is not *on* earth, so much as *in* earth!" He was obviously pleased with his little joke. He continued: "The water, when it emerges, is hot. There is no need for us to wait until it is cool, so we collect natural herbs and fruit that grow in our forest, and place them in the water. I'm afraid I don't know anything about the process. There are some that do, and we leave it to them." He placed his empty glass on a nearby table. "That's enough before dinner."

Cecil then led them into another grand room, where a long table stood in the centre, with rows of chairs placed down each side. The cats were almost too overwhelmed to sit down, but they were overcome by hunger.

Cecil sat at the head of the table, flanked by the Captain and his wife, then Jabez and his officers, and of course Uncle Ebenezer, who was looking very closely at the big bowl of flowers in the centre of the table. Many of them were strange to him, and he had taken out his pocket book to make notes of them. He could hardly wait for the next day, when he would be out early, seriously seeking for the rare flowers to be found on the island.

The rest of the places at the table were filled with the crew of the 'Jabez', and by a selected number of Bouncers.

After a short speech of welcome, Cecil rang a bell which was placed by his right hand, whereupon a small procession, headed by Boris, entered the room, carrying large silver dishes. These were accompanied by a delicious smell.

Deftly, Boris and his staff placed upon each plate four golden fish, served with a special sauce. To the hungry crew, it didn't seem much of a meal! Cecil guessed what was in their minds.

"Don't worry! This is only the first course, just to get you in the mood for eating." This was good news, and soon they had cleared their plates.

The procession, again led by Boris, re-entered the room, this time with even larger dishes. Prior to their appearance, the glasses had been filled. Jabez noticed that Cecil's glass was almost constantly empty!

With a flourish, the dish covers were removed, whereupon cheers rang out from the cats. "It's bangers and mash!" they cried. What a great surprise – a dish loved by great and small throughout the world!

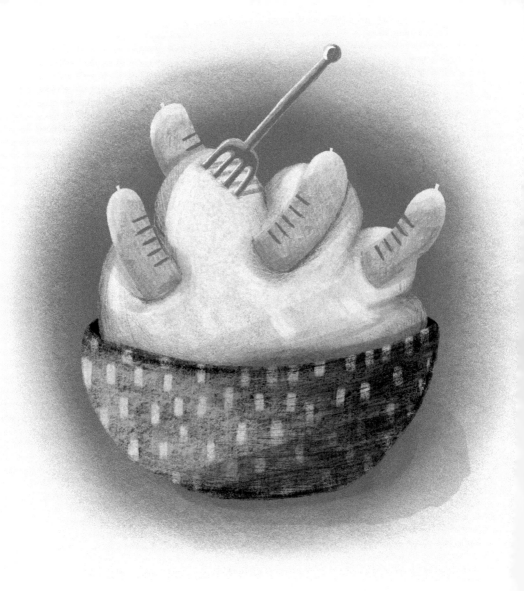

Cecil confided to Captain Catte, "The sausages have been made from the meat tree I told you about. And we grow the potatoes ourselves, very successfully."

"I'm not surprised by anything you tell me, Cecil," said Mrs Jones. "This place is the nearest I shall ever get to heaven. You all seem so happy here. Does anyone ever have an argument?"

Captain Catte agreed with what his wife had said, but he wished to know more.

"Do you mind if I ask you some questions, Cecil?" he enquired. "I'm keen to know all about you."

Cecil waved an expansive arm. "Delighted, old boy! Ask me whatever you want to know. Fire away, my friend."

"Well, to start with, how on earth did you build so fine a house, and furnish it with articles which have been made by supreme craftsmen?"

Cecil shook his head. "We didn't."

Captain Catte was puzzled. "How do you mean, you didn't?"

"We didn't build the house or make the furniture," explained Cecil. "It has been here as long as any of us can remember. Once upon a time there must have been a rich settlement here. They might have come from across the seas, to escape from some kind of disaster. We just don't know. However, they left behind most of the things you see that are so beautifully made. Not only the furniture, but cutlery, plates and glasses."

Cecil paused to take a drink of wine, then continued: "We have been lucky. There is a large library, and we all read a lot. I am interested in history."

Chapter 10

I T WAS NOW Captain Catte's turn.
"Please don't think me rude or personal, but just what is your position in the settlement? You must be someone of importance?" He waved his hand at all the signs of wealth.

Cecil smiled kindly at the Captain. "I don't mind your questions," he said. "I suppose that at the moment, I could be said to be important, but probably not in the way you mean. This is not my house, and these are not my belongings. They are shared by everyone who lives on the island. I am the Governor. It's my turn, you see.

"During my year in office, I am responsible for organising the farming, fishing, and other activities. If there happen to be any disputes, it's my job to get them settled. As there is no form of money here, there is not much cause for upsets. It's all very democratic. When anything does arise, it is usually of minor importance and is soon put right."

Cecil paused for a moment. "Even the cottages are built on similar lines. If a family increases, we just add a bit on. This house, of course, is different, but is evenly shared among my fellows. When my year is up, another takes my place. Everyone gets a chance to live here. Some, of course, have no desire to. There are always people who don't want responsibility."

Cecil leaned back and studied his glass with disfavour. It was less than half full.

"I hope you know more about us now," he said, "but we don't know much about you, particularly what you intend to do here."

Captain Catte decided it was time to tell their story.

"Of course we will tell you just what brought us here! It is quite a plain story. Uncle Ebenezer here" – he turned and motioned to his Uncle sitting near – "is an expert on rare flowers throughout the world, and has spent his time reading books and getting information wherever possible. But, as he says, merely reading about plants is not the same as actually seeing them."

"So, for this reason," Captain Catte continued, "we have come to your island so that he may study your rare plant life. I hope that this is agreeable to you, Cecil?"

"Yes, by all means, Uncle Ebenezer!" exclaimed Cecil with delight. "How very interesting! And some of my Bouncers must go with you, so that they can tell you where particular types of plants are to be found."

Both Uncle Ebenezer and Captain Catte were warm in their thanks for Cecil's kindness, and Uncle began to make plans for an early start on the next day's exploration.

The wonderful meal came to an end at last, and all – particularly the visitors – decided that they should settle down for the night.

Many of the cats could hardly believe all that had taken place that day. But it didn't matter, for soon they were fast asleep!

Chapter 11

CAPTAIN CATTE WAS up early, only to find that Uncle Ebenezer was already gone, accompanied by two Bouncers. As the Captain gazed with pleasure across the bay below him, a party of lady Bouncers made their way up the slope of the volcano, carrying wooden buckets and little stools. He was curious.

"Where are you all going?" he asked them.

"Why, milking, of course!" replied one. "You may join us if you wish."

The Captain had heard that goats could be bad-tempered, and that they had horns! He declined, saying that it wasn't really something he was interested in.

"But I do know someone who would be tickled to go with you," he said. "It's our Mrs Jones. May I ask her?"

They were more than pleased to invite her, and the Captain went off to tell her. As he left her, he was joined by Cecil.

"I know you intend to leave us as soon as Uncle Ebenezer has finished his search for unknown plants, but tomorrow is our sports day. You may have noticed the white lines and hurdles on the green." Captain Catte nodded, and Cecil continued, "Well, how would you like to join in? Could be fun, don't you think?"

By now Jabez had joined them, and he turned to the Captain.

"'Twould keep the crew out of mischief, sir," he said, "and

stop 'em getting stale. I thinks us should take them Bouncers on."

Captain Catte could see the wisdom of this and readily agreed, saying that it would be a good ending to their stay with Cecil and his people.

So it was that, in the early morning, the astonished cats were shaken out of their sleep and told what was expected of them. They were not amused! Cats do not like getting out of bed early – they prefer to lie in. Of course, nights are different – that's when they do their hunting.

It was clear to the Captain that in many events, the Bouncers held an advantage, because they were elastic. For this reason, a rule was made that no Bouncer could change shape once the sports had begun. There were some moans about this, but these were ignored.

Both teams were fairly equal, so that the contest was evenly balanced. Much to their surprise, the cats were enjoying themselves, even though they were, at the end, one event down.

"What a shame!" cried Cecil. "Nobody deserves to lose!"

"Hold on – not so fast, me hearty!" It was Jabez. "There's one more thing us have to do before 'tis over! A tug of war!"

"What in heaven's name is a tug of war?" asked Cecil. He had never heard of it, so Jabez explained and the Bouncers were fascinated. They demanded that it should take place.

So, a rope was fetched, the two teams lined up, and the teams strained until their faces were red, while the two Captains cheered their respective teams on.

The Bouncers were good, but not good enough, as the cats used their claws to good effect on the ground. Slowly the rope went in favour of Jabez's crew, and with one last heave they won!

Cecil was overjoyed. "Bravo, bravo!" he cried. "What a great sport, and we're level, so it's a draw!"

"A fair result," agreed the Captain, then delivered his own surprise. "We have an invitation to you all. We have prepared a meal for you down by the 'Jabez', as a farewell token of our friendship and gratitude."

With a cheer, everyone rushed down to the quayside, where the day ended in style. A magnificent dinner had been prepared, together with ale brought from Merridew. Cecil in particular found it to his liking!

When the sun set, a tired but happy band made their way to bed. The morning was going to bring their return on the 'Jabez'.

Chapter 12

THEY AWOKE REFRESHED, and hungry. A large breakfast had been prepared for them, which they attacked with relish. Afterwards, they were taken on the tour of the settlement, which had been promised by Cecil.

What they saw made their eyes pop out with surprise. In front of them was a blue lake surrounded by green parkland. Here and there were log cabins, some shaded by clumps of trees. There were beds of brightly coloured flowers everywhere.

On the edge of the lake were drawn up rows of little boats, all painted in different hues. Captain Catte looked at it in wonder!

"Hard to take in, isn't it?" asked Cecil, watching him.

"It certainly is!" said the Captain.

"What's it for?" put in Jabez.

"It's a holiday village," replied Cecil. "I manage the project, but all the community benefits from any profits."

Captain Catte was most impressed.

"I do wish I'd heard of this earlier. Maybe I could have joined you," he said regretfully.

"My dear chap," said Cecil, nodding his head vigorously. "We'd be delighted to have you with us at any time. Why, you might be able to suggest some improvements!"

"I don't think it can be any better than it is already, but I have an idea to put to you."

"Fire away, Captain," said Cecil enthusiastically.

"All right." The Captain paused. "How about a cheese factory?"

Cecil seemed doubtful. "Do you think it would be popular? And where would the milk come from? Our goats aren't numerous enough, I'm afraid."

"From our cows brought from Merridew. The factory I have in mind could have side-shows to amuse the holidaymakers!"

Cecil grinned. In his mind the plan was taking shape.

"We must get down to details, have some meetings!"

But there the project rested for the time being. Captain Catte and his crew had been a long time away from their families and friends in Merridew, but they all agreed they would return before long, to renew their friendship with the Bouncers.

CAPTAIN CATTE
AND
RED JAKE
THE PIRATE

Chapter 1

CAPTAIN CATTE JUST couldn't understand it! As he approached the quay he peered out to sea. He was watching a ship which had appeared on the horizon. It didn't seem to be a Merridew ship, and it looked to be in some distress. Its course was erratic, and as it drew closer, only a few men could be seen on deck – certainly not enough to handle it.

She was carrying far too much sail, and was speeding straight for the breakwater of the harbour!

By now, a large crowd had gathered around the Captain, and they watched in horror as the ship raced onwards. A collision was certain! But at the last moment, one of the crew must have managed to alter the ship's course, for it veered off to port, making for the beach instead of the harbour wall.

It hit with a force so great that the masts snapped, hurling sails, spars, and rigging over the sides!

For a moment there was shocked silence, then Captain Catte and the crowd with him rushed down to the beach to see what they could do. At first, there didn't seem to be any survivors, but a careful search revealed four of the crew alive – but only just.

Gently, the poor souls were carried up to a cottage owned by Captain Jabez, reputed to be the wisest fisherman of them all. He volunteered to care for them, and to inform Captain Catte when they were in a fit state to talk.

The survivors were utterly exhausted, and it was some time before they began to recover. At once Jabez sent for Captain Catte, who was anxious to interview them. He rushed to their bedsides.

One of them was a mate of the wrecked ship, and it was a very strange story he had to tell.

Chapter 2

"**O**UR SHIP WAS a trader," the mate told those who had crowded round to listen to him. "Whenever we reach our destination, the Captain goes ashore – always the Captain, with one of the officers and a couple of the crew members. Anyway," he continued, "this last time, off he went with his party, whilst the rest of us stayed aboard. He and his party haven't been seen since!"

He paused for a moment, to take a drink which Captain Catte put to his lips, then he continued.

"We waited for several hours, but when there was still no sign of them, we decided we'd better go and search. The four of us rowed for the cove where they had landed, and pulled the boat up out of reach of any tides. We made for the trading post, but all the huts were empty, and nobody was about. In the main building we found that tables and chairs were overturned, showing that a violent struggle had taken place. There were also traces of blood!"

The sailor shivered with fear. "Suddenly, behind us came a ghastly loud shout. We turned in horror! Facing us was a terrible man – he was enormous, but it was his ugly face that was so frightening. He was swarthy, with wild red hair, a big thick beard to match and a patch worn over his left eye. But what made him even more fearsome was his right eye... deep red, piercing through you like a torch!"

A gasp came from Jabez. "Red Jake!" he whispered. "It must have been Red Jake! One of the worst pirates ever to curse the seas!"

Captain Catte looked doubtful. "D'you really think so, Jabez? After all, he'd be very old by now, wouldn't he?"

"Not so, Captain," said Jabez, "'ee started out as a pirate when 'ee was very young, and I've seen 'im. I wouldn't have forgotten 'im, I can assure you." He turned back to the mate. "What did you do?"

The mate whispered, as though afraid that Red Jake might hear him.

"Well, this great giant yelled at us, telling us he was going to get us, like he'd got our shipmates. We were dead scared, and seeing how we couldn't escape past him through the doorway, we leapt through the nearest window and ran for our boat. We could hear him roaring his gang on behind us, but somehow, we made it to the beach and rowed for the ship. We hoisted the sails like madmen and made it to sea."

The mate had at last come to the end of his story, and everyone in the room was quiet, trying to imagine what it must have been like, sailing the ship with only four pairs of hands instead of the full crew!

"If it hadn't been for the courage of the mate," Jabez mused, "they be perished for sure."

Chapter 3

CAPTAIN CATTE, HEAD in hand, sat and thought about the mate's story. He realised that, according to his account, the Captain and his party had been kidnapped by Red Jake and his gang, and were being held captive. At length, he decided that it was up to him and his friends to find and release them from the pirate's clutches. His first step must be to call an urgent meeting of all the cats in Merridew at their special ancient 'meeting tree'. His tried and trusted assistant, Sinbad the crow, flew around, his raucous voice telling everyone to attend Captain Catte's important meeting.

Soon the Captain stood before a large crowd of cats, and when he was satisfied that they were all present, he addressed them in a commanding voice.

"Friends," he began, "I have been thinking about the survivors of the unfortunate 'Matilda', which came aground on the beach. Now, somewhere, its Captain and some of its crew are being held prisoner, and it's pretty certain that the notorious pirate, Red Jake, is behind it all."

He paused in order to let that sink in, then continued firmly.

"I want to find out where they are, then I propose to mount a rescue. Now, who's with me?"

A roar went up from the gathered crowd, and Captain Catte said, "I suppose I can take it that you're all behind me in this venture?"

There was another shout of agreement, and the cats pressed close to him, shaking his hand and pledging their full support for his plan.

With great enthusiasm, they set about making preparations for their adventure. They were to set sail on the good ship 'Jabez', and her owner, Captain Jabez, organised all the workers, who were a very able ship's crew. Needless to say, they couldn't wait for the day when they would put to sea and sail for the island off distant Africa, where – according to the mate of the 'Matilda' – its Captain and some of the crew were held prisoner by Red Jake.

At length, all the preparations were finished, and all that was needed was fair weather, and this came soon. All the villagers crammed the quay, each one waving, and many wishing that they too were going with the adventurers.

The 'Jabez' slid silently from the quay, with her sails slowly filling. At last they were on their way.

Chapter 4

DAY AFTER DAY, the stout little ship ploughed her way through the ocean, with all sails set for maximum speed, on their way to Africa and the island which they had never visited before.

The two Captains took turns around the decks, organising each day's duties. At last, one day came the cry of "Sail ho!" from the look-out up in the crow's nest at the top of one of the masts.

Captain Catte gazed in the direction to which the sailor was pointing. Sure enough, just above the horizon he could see sails appear. On the bridge, Captain Jabez put his telescope to his eye and studied the approaching vessel.

"Well, she's fast, judging by the bow wave," he observed.

"They've seen us, 'cause they've come around to our tack."

Captain Catte took the telescope and watched closely as the distance between the two ships continued to narrow. Suddenly he stiffened.

"Quick, Jabez! Take a look at that flag she's just hoisted!"

Jabez glared through the glass and, in a voice of dread, muttered, "'tis the skull and crossbones! 'Er's a pirate!" He spun round to the helmsman. "Hard to starboard!" he cried, then turned again to Captain Catte. "Us'll have to run before 'em – 'tis our only chance! We'll get more speed if us rigs up some extra canvas."

He bellowed his order to the mate, and soon the crew were running up the rigging to hoist extra sails.

"If us can keep our distance until dark," explained Jabez, "then us can alter our course and escape 'em during the night, but 'tis going to be a close run thing!"

Suddenly a loud crack sounded from the pirate ship. A puff of smoke was seen, followed by a plume of water behind the 'Jabez'.

"They're firing at us!" shouted Captain Catte. "But don't worry, men – we're well out of range at present. My guess is that they're trying to frighten us into stopping."

"That's right," agreed Jabez. "If we keep our heads and wait 'til dark, then us'll be safe. Just you trust Captain Catte and me!"

The pirates loosed off several more rounds, but all fell short. The crew took heart from this, but they were still being chased and couldn't slacken their speed.

Gradually daylight slipped away into a deep dark blue, and in no time it was night. They could no longer see their pursuers, for there was no moon, which was ideal for an escape attempt.

Jabez gathered the crew around him and very quietly gave his orders.

"Up aloft, lads!" he said. "We must take in some sail and reduce our speed." Captain Catte was puzzled. While he didn't want to disagree with Jabez, at the same time he felt that to slow down was the last thing they ought to be doing. He leant towards Jabez and whispered, "What's your thinking, Jabez?"

"If us keeps up this rate," explained Jabez quietly, "although 'tis a dark night, they'll be able to see our wake. 'Tis wide and luminous – stands out a mile it does! If us stays on this speed, they'll catch us for sure, have no fear of that. But if us reduces our speed, then makes a hard turn to port, us'll almost certainly lose 'em."

Captain Catte looked at Jabez with great respect. Without him, they would undoubtedly have fallen victim to the pirates.

The ship glided through the water like a spectre. Not a ripple could be seen, nor a sound heard above a whisper or two. They could hear the shouts and curses of their enemies, as sound travels great distances over water, yet even those noises faded away – as did the pirates – who hadn't altered course.

Chapter 5

AFTER SEVERAL HOURS, Jabez stepped forward, straining his eyes and ears. There was now no sound but that of their own passage.

"Us now be out of danger, Captain!" he said cheerfully.

On his orders, the rest of the sails were furled, and a sea anchor streamed, so that they almost came to a halt. He didn't know the seas they were in, so there was the danger of their being driven ashore – it would be wise to wait for daylight before continuing on their way.

Fearfully they awaited the dawn, praying that when it did come there would be no pirate ship to be seen.

They need not have worried. The sea was empty, and there was no sighting of land. They could safely continue their voyage, so all sail was set and they began to make up for lost time, putting as much distance as possible between themselves and the pirates.

After several days, Captain Catte raised his head and sniffed the air. Cats have a very strong sense of smell.

"I believe we're getting near to some land," he said. "I can smell trees!"

This was soon confirmed by a cry of "Land ho!" from the masthead, and the lookout pointed ahead.

They rushed to the bows and, sure enough, a dark line stretched across the horizon. They cruised slowly towards the land. As they came nearer, they could make out dense forests, above which rose a volcano with smoke issuing from its summit.

"This may be an island," remarked Jabez. "Us'll take the ship round a bit and see whether there's good anchorage. Them pirates may come this way and if possible us wants the ship to be out of sight."

Jabez was right – it was indeed an island, and they came upon a sheltered cove, well hidden from prying eyes. A crewman was placed in the bows to sound the depths as the ship inched into the little natural harbour. At last, Jabez was satisfied, and they dropped anchor.

The longboat was launched and a small party, led by Captain Catte, made for the shore. The boat grounded on the sands and they disembarked. Before them was opened up a most beautiful place. They walked through forests of tall trees, beneath which grew exotic plants, riotous with gorgeous colours. Overhead, the warm sun shone.

Captain Catte sighed contentedly.

"This is heaven on earth," he said. Then he closed his eyes and offered a prayer of thanks for their safe journey across the ocean.

Chapter 6

NOW PATROLS WERE sent further into the interior of the island to find a suitable site for their camp. Captain Catte himself wandered along the tide line, noting its limits, so that they stood in no danger of losing their boat through carelessness.

On their return, the patrols reported finding a grassy clearing in the forest, with a stream of clear water running through it. This was good news, especially as there had been no signs of any creatures or habitation. This information was sent back to the ship and Jabez set about getting the crew ashore, leaving just a small party on board as guard.

Captain Catte then put them all to work building a camp. There was much to do in erecting suitable shelters and, to be on the safe side, he devised a system of defences, so trenches had to be dug.

By now, the crew were tired and hungry so, after a good meal, they dragged themselves off to bed, except, of course, for those who were to be on guard duty during the night.

The next morning, Captain Catte was awakened by the songs of birds and the warming rays of the rising sun.

There was much to be done, and the Captain held a conference with Captain Jabez.

"Did you notice those goats in the distance yesterday?" Captain Catte asked Jabez. "I suggest we go up into the mountains and seek them – they will be useful for their milk. And as I think this is the right island, according to the description given by the mate of the wrecked 'Matilda', we must keep a close lookout for signs of the pirates who kidnapped the Captain and several of his crew."

It was a long march, but the thought of goats and fresh milk – which they loved! – spurred them on.

Everything seemed perfect, yet Captain Catte felt uneasy. He turned to Jabez.

"You know, I'm not sure what it is," he said quietly, "but something's worrying me. I have a strange feeling that we're being watched!"

Jabez looked at the Captain in amazement.

"Well, I'm blessed!" he said. "I've had the same notion myself, but I didn't want to say anything. I always knows when there's trouble brewing, and my instinct has never let me down."

The Captain nodded in agreement. "Better keep it to ourselves, eh? We don't want to start a panic."

So they continued their march, moving carefully through the undergrowth, until the Captain whispered suddenly, "There's someone on the footpath!" He was right. On his whispered command, they all lay still, and a dark shape passed by their hiding-place. A guard!

They gave him time to get clear – he obviously suspected nothing – then they moved on.

Chapter 7

EVENTUALLY THEY CAME to a strong barricade, over which they could see no sign of life from the compound nearby.

After a whispered discussion, Captain Catte and Jabez decided to attack the pirates, in the hope of finding the sailors who had been kidnapped.

They were all suffering from butterflies in their tummies. Most folk do when they are approaching danger. Quietly, they all climbed over the boundary fence, first stopping at the top while Captain Catte listened.

Still, there was no sign of activity and, at a word of command from the Captain, they dropped to the ground on the far side.

They decided that they must push forward and attack, but as it turned out, it wasn't like an attack – there were no enemies!

Jabez was uneasy. "Doesn't feel right," he muttered. "I've got a nasty feeling even more strongly now!"

"So have I," admitted the Captain. "Something is wrong, very wrong." But it was no good – they had to get on with their efforts to find and free the missing seamen.

They had to cross a stretch of open ground which was now bathed in moonlight. The Captain led the way.

Suddenly he felt himself falling! He ended up in a very deep trench, and all around him was his party of cats. They had been trapped! And this was only the start of their troubles, for without warning, great nets flew down on top of them. They were powerless to avoid them.

"Don't struggle!" yelled the Captain. "That will only make matters worse. We've been ambushed." He spoke to Jabez, who lay beside him. "I've made a real mess of it! I should have known that it was all too easy." Jabez tried to reassure him, but to no avail. As the Captain said, he was the leader, and should have known better.

For a long time, the crew lay trapped in the ditch, waiting for something to happen, but nothing did. The sun rose, and with it the heat increased. This brought fresh misery, for no one had taken food or drink for a long time.

Captain Catte was very worried for his men, who must be as distressed as he. And of course, there was no hope of escape – despite their efforts to free themselves from beneath the net which enveloped them, they had been unsuccessful.

Chapter 8

ABOUT MID-MORNING A shadow fell across the Captain. He looked up. Above him towered someone who could be none other than Red Jake!

He grinned evilly down on them.

"Well, well! Here's a pretty how-de-do, ain't it, Captain Catte? Fancy you falling into such a simple trap! And you being so clever!" Then he scowled, making him even more ugly. "I've heard a lot about you, but never thought I'd have such a good chance to capture you."

Captain Catte was no coward. Even in his present plight, he was defiant.

"It's not yet over, Jake – of that you can be sure! And now if you've finished enjoying the sound of your own voice, just what do you intend to do?"

Jake growled. "Brave words come easy. You won't escape! You can put that aside for a start – you won't be given a chance."

"Come on, you great leader of men!" the Captain snarled at him. "Cut the talk and let's see what you can really do!"

By now, the rest of the pirates were lining the top of the trench, grinning at the prospect of some fun. Red Jake was not at all put out by the Captain's sarcasm. "You'll soon see what I can do! And while you think about what that might be, we'll have you all in chains, for safety's sake."

With this, he gave his orders to his men, who lifted them

one by one from the trench and chained their arms and feet. They were then attached to each other by one long chain.

"I've a special plan for you, Captain Catte," he promised evilly, then ordered the prisoners to be led off to a large hut by the side of the clearing. The hut had no windows, and the door was firmly bolted on the outside. To make matters worse, they were still given no food or water.

Poor Captain Catte was in despair. What an end to their efforts to release the captured seamen! Fancy his having fallen victim to such a trick. His life would be forfeit, as well as the lives of all his crew.

He knew all about Red Jake's vicious character, and could expect no mercy. He wished with all his heart that they were back in the peace and safety of Merridew.

The day wore on. It became cooler, and this brought the captives some relief. Towards evening, the door opened and some of the pirates entered, carrying plates of bread and jugs of water. This was a great relief to Captain Catte and his men, who had come to the conclusion that they were to be starved to death!

As nothing more seemed to be happening, they decided that they might as well go to sleep. This they did, despite the hard floor on which they lay.

Early the next morning, they heard footsteps marching towards their hut. Captain Catte wondered what was to be done to his crew. He was fearful for their safety. It didn't occur to him to worry about himself – his men were more important.

Chapter 9

THE DOOR WAS unbolted and thrown open. Outside was a party of fierce, heavily-armed pirates. "Out you lot come!" snarled one of them, apparently the leader. The guards formed up on either side of the prisoners, the leader placing himself at the head of the column.

Captain Catte wondered what was now going to be their fate. Were they all to lose their lives? It was a dreadful thought, to be in the hands of such evil men.

They were led across the clearing through a belt of trees which gave way to a large square. In the bright sunshine, the Captain could see the men who had been captured from the 'Matilda' as well as Captain Jabez, and his own crew all still in chains.

The Captain was not faint-hearted, but it was obvious that he was going to be the reason for this parade.

It was an execution – his!

There was complete silence – no sound, even from his own men. Then, in the distance, a drum began to beat. It was muffled and slow.

Captain Catte's fears were realised. A small group came into view, following the drummer. With them was Red Jake, as frightening as ever, with his shaggy red hair and beard, and piercing red eye. They came to a halt in front of the Captain.

Red Jake spoke. He raised his voice, which was surprisingly

solemn, so that it would be heard by pirates and captives alike.

"You all know my feelings towards Captain Catte here. He is my worst enemy. There will be a settling between us in front of you all. I intend that we shall fight a duel!" He turned to Captain Catte.

"Whatever the result should be, I swear that you and your crew and those others who are my captives will be set free."

Red Jake motioned one of the pirates to come forward. He was carrying an ornate wooden box, which Jake took from him.

"In this casket there are two duelling weapons," he said. "I will admit that it is my favourite choice, so I will have an advantage. However, you shall take your pick. That is as fair as I intend to be."

He raised his voice again so that all could hear.

"The Captain has been a worthy opponent, and brave, so I promise him, in front of you all, a dignified funeral, and the freedom of all his men."

He opened the box, held it towards the Captain, and demanded, "Choose your weapon!"

The Captain looked inside the box. He couldn't believe what he was seeing. He was speechless... was this some sort of joke?

Before he could utter a single word, Red Jake and all the pirates exploded into uncontrollable laughter. Inside the box were two very long cucumbers!

"Captain Catte!" growled Red Jake. "You have been such a thorn in my side for a long, long time and I had considered taking this opportunity to dispose of you for good. But it grieves me to say that I have actually come to respect and admire you and, yes, we *will* duel together – but with these cucumbers! And – " he chuckled, "I promise to keep my word that whatever the outcome of this 'deadly' contest between us, all of you will go free."

With such relief, Captain Catte chose his cucumber, and Jake took the other. "En-guarde!" Jake joked.

Even though they were fighting with cucumbers, Captain Catte was determined to put on a good performance in front of his men, and he knew his nimbleness would allow him to run rings around the huge, cumbersome pirate. He was very careful, however, not to intimidate Jake, or show him up, for fear of making him change his mind. The two of them played out this charade with all the pirates and former captives clapping and cheering.

As the Captain and Jake continued to swap thrusts for parries, Red Jake suddenly shouted: "Stop, that's enough. Let's party instead!" With that, his men appeared, carrying flagons of drinks, huge platters of food and laid the whole lot out for everyone to help themselves. They all partied well into the night and fell asleep very relieved compared with what might have been.

Next morning, Captain Catte assembled his men, together with the liberated captain and sailors from the 'Matilda'. As a mark of professionalism, Captain Catte offered his hand to Red Jake and the two of them shook respectfully and bade farewell. They would never be best of friends, but there was a mutual understanding between them.

Their ship 'Jabez' awaited Captain Catte and all the men. Thankful for such an unexpected outcome, they set sail on the long voyage back to Merridew. A happy end to yet another adventure.

From this day, peace and happiness reigned in Merridew.

Ingram Content Group UK Ltd.
Milton Keynes UK
UKHW050006140323
418425UK00018B/126

9 781528 931143